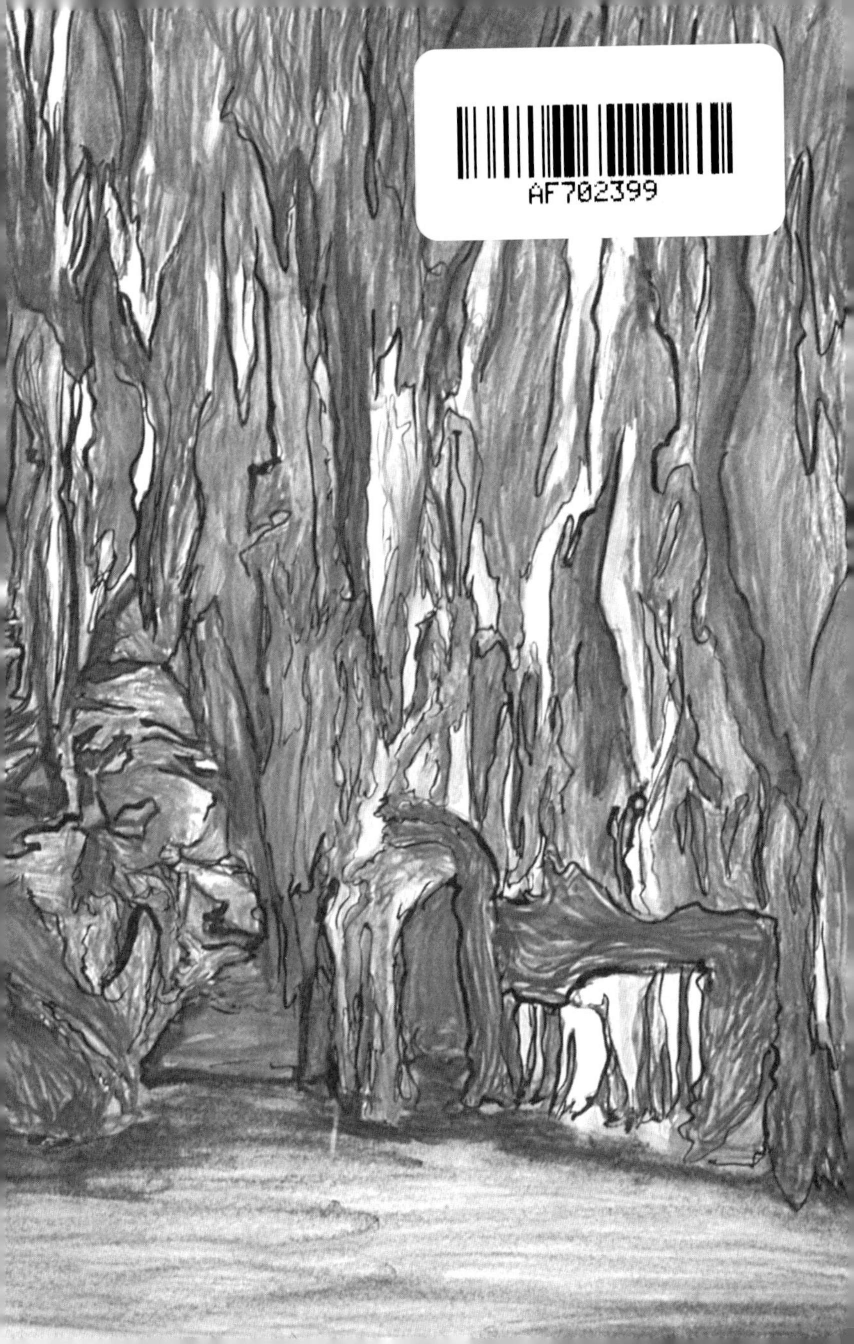

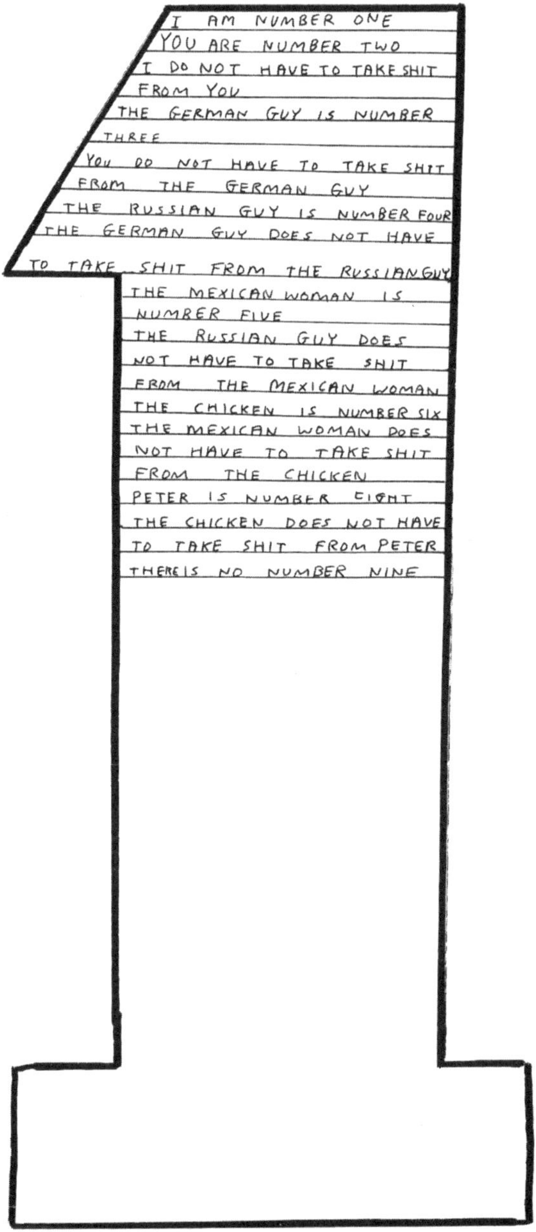
I AM NUMBER ONE
YOU ARE NUMBER TWO
I DO NOT HAVE TO TAKE SHIT
FROM YOU
THE GERMAN GUY IS NUMBER
THREE
YOU DO NOT HAVE TO TAKE SHIT
FROM THE GERMAN GUY
THE RUSSIAN GUY IS NUMBER FOUR
THE GERMAN GUY DOES NOT HAVE
TO TAKE SHIT FROM THE RUSSIAN GUY
THE MEXICAN WOMAN IS
NUMBER FIVE
THE RUSSIAN GUY DOES
NOT HAVE TO TAKE SHIT
FROM THE MEXICAN WOMAN
THE CHICKEN IS NUMBER SIX
THE MEXICAN WOMAN DOES
NOT HAVE TO TAKE SHIT
FROM THE CHICKEN
PETER IS NUMBER EIGHT
THE CHICKEN DOES NOT HAVE
TO TAKE SHIT FROM PETER
THERE IS NO NUMBER NINE

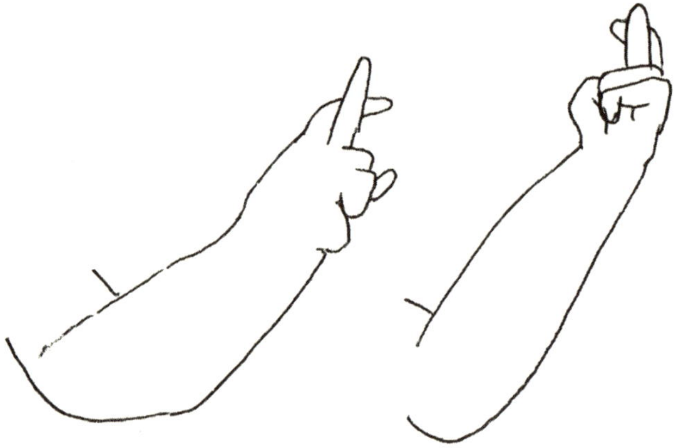

J&L ILLUSTRATED #2

Fiction commissioned and edited by Craig Taylor
Drawings commissioned and edited by Leanne Shapton and Jason Fulford

Contact J&L by mail at P.O. Box 723991 Atlanta, GA, USA 31139

ISBN 0-9746908-2-1
Printed in Iceland

Front cover: Leanne Shapton
Back cover: Jason Logan
Front Endpages: Amy O'Neill
Back Endpages: Leanne Shapton

FICTION

DRAWINGS

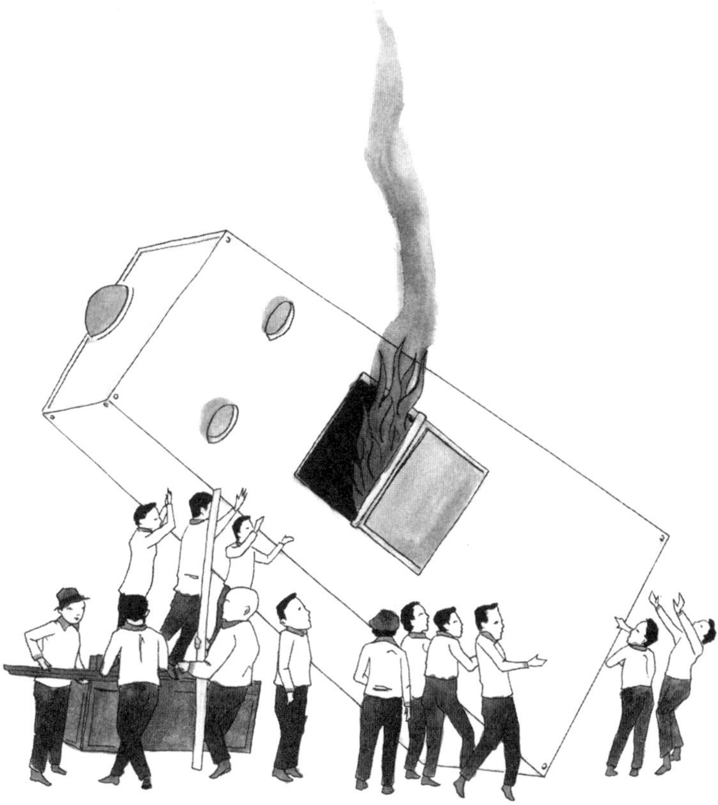

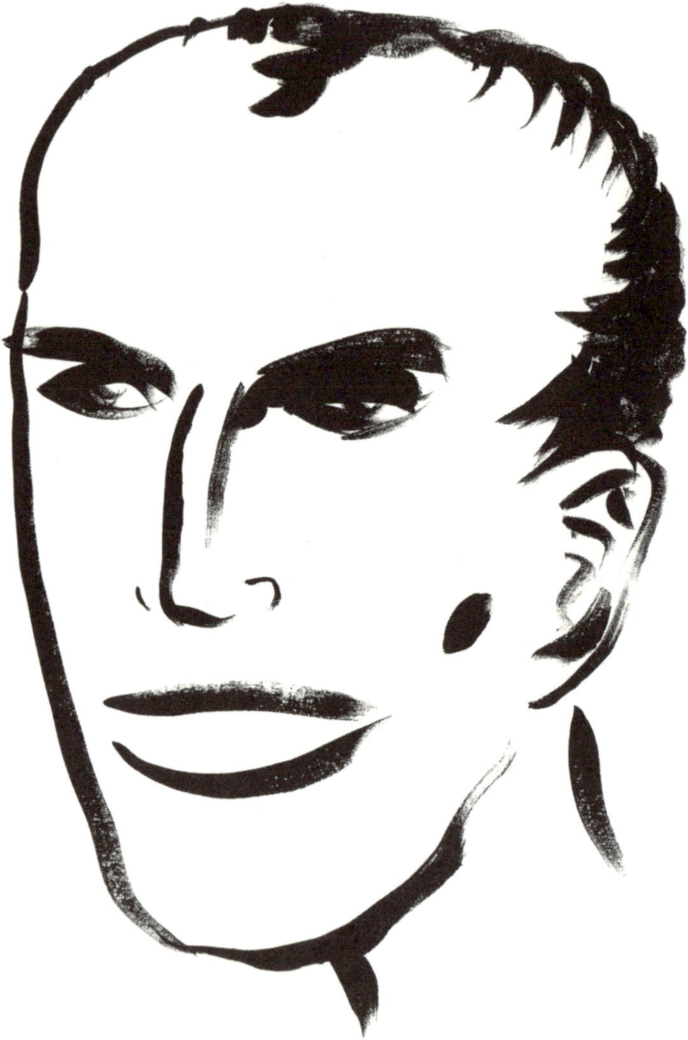

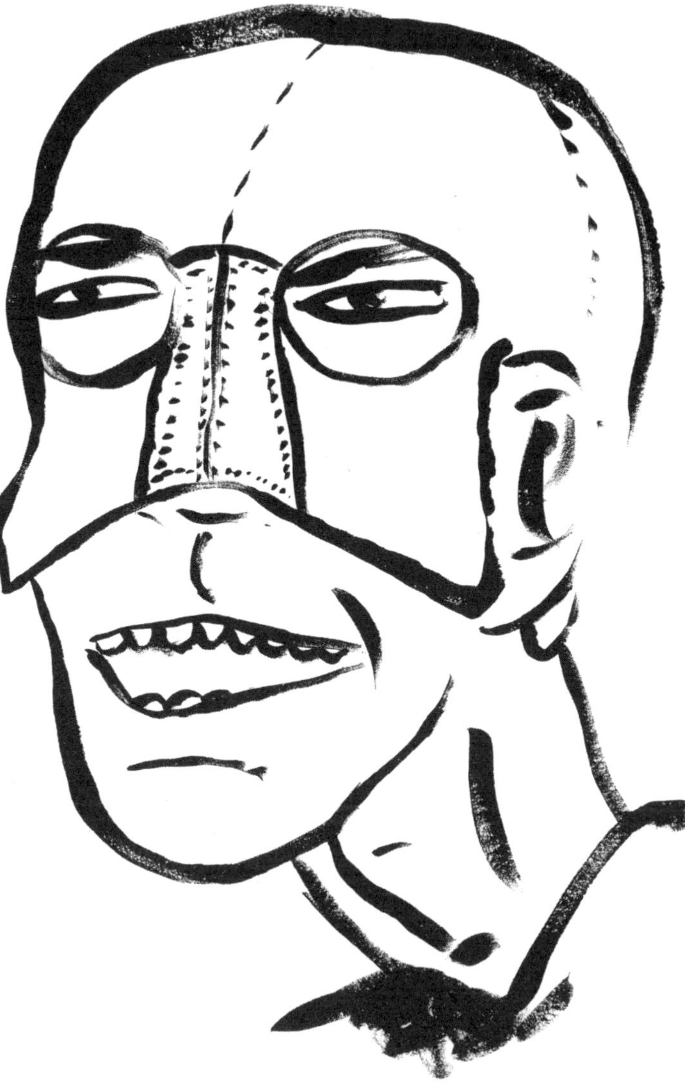

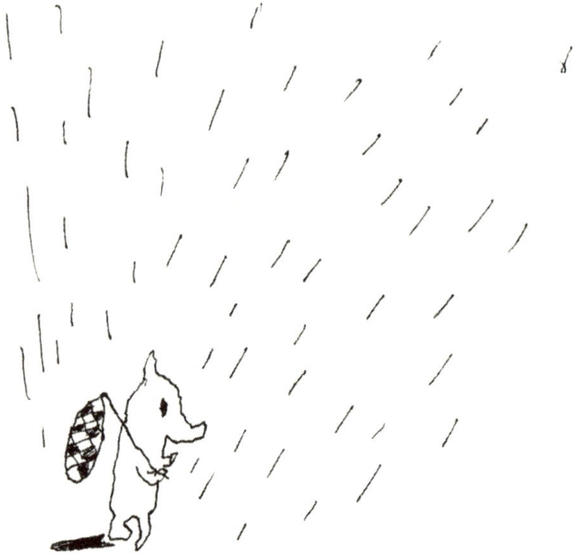

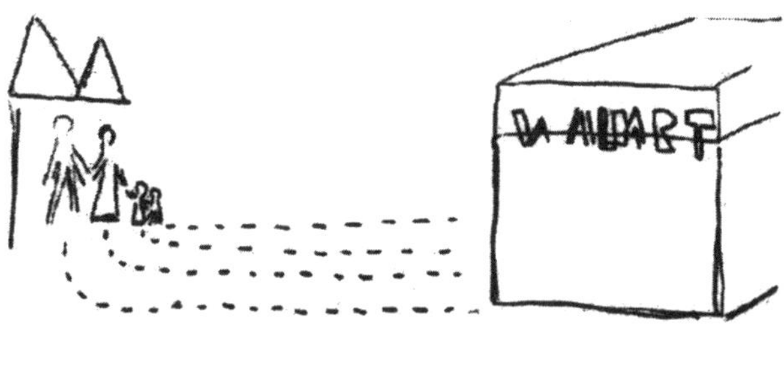

Editor's Note

The theme of this collection of short stories is Adventure. A few months ago, I answered a posting at my local Job Centre. A small company was looking for someone to edit their new book. During my job interview I made one thing clear to the publishers. I wanted this book to be populated by killers, cowboys, superheroes, and eerie happenings. It certainly is.

This book was very interesting to edit, especially for someone like myself. I don't edit fiction, nor do I write fiction, and I don't read fiction either. I like business. The last book I read was the biography of successful Canadian businessman Jimmy Pattison, who started a chain of grocery stores after making millions with his car dealerships. I was let down by the ending, when stock prices plummeted and Pattison refused to take advantage of the potential of in-store bakeries, so I have endeavored to make the ending of this particular book far better. And funnier. You won't leave disappointed, which, as you might recall, was the slogan of Jimmy Pattison's car dealerships.

This book was edited during an intense two-week period in the winter of 2003 on Protection Island, a small dot off the coast of Vancouver Island, in Canada. On the advice of other, more experienced fiction editors, I used a very sharp red pencil to make changes. I kept five pencils in my small bedroom, or 'editing suite', so the process could continue unhindered. My editing routine went something like this: Each day I woke promptly at seven, I started the woodstove, made suggestions of what my mother might prepare for lunch—the house belongs to her—then I walked down the dirt roads to the dock to see if the first ferry had delivered any new drafts from the writers. After seeing off the ferry I stopped in at my friend Keith's place to look through his telescope at the freighters that were anchored in the strait off the shore of the island. Keith has a telescope so powerful you can sometimes see the seamen moving on the ship's decks. Even though he's in his late forties, Keith doesn't believe in steady employment. Instead he owns at least twenty notebooks full of the names of different ships that pass by, complete with their corresponding home countries, so each day we check each ship against his books, then the country, then talk about the role that country played in World War Two, particularly in the oceanic theatres of war, which makes spotting Japanese freighters great because it gives me a chance to recount some facts about the tactical importance of Saipan in WW2 and Keith a chance to take a few slices at the arbutus trees outside his house with the Japanese samurai sword he bought in November. The sword was a bad choice, business-wise, because the price would have inevitably fallen in January in line with the post-Christmas slump. Regardless, Keith's sword is utterly amazing. It takes chunks out of arbutus trees the size and texture of a thawed filet of fish from McDonald's. (Perhaps this would be a good time to mention that before editing this book I was manager at the Rutherford Mall McDonald's, which under my stewardship became top grosser in sales in Vancouver Island and was ranked thirteenth in the province.)

By 11:45am I was back home and ready for a day spent editing fiction. At noon my mother knocked and announced lunch. A note about my mother: On the day I answered the job posting we made a deal. While I was editing this book she promised to clean out the spare room. This was not just a question of just making the bed. She would have to take care of her collection of newspaper clippings that were stacked in some places higher than my head. I could never find out what made her keep these clippings – recipes, small biographies of people I had known from high school, obituaries of old miners. Anchoring the lower levels of the stacks were *National Geographics* and *Chatelaines*. Unfortunately, tucked away amidst the clippings were photos of the family, so the archaeological dig had to be done with care and consideration. Each sheath of paper was lifted, examined, and then consigned to the woodstove.

Just today, I decided I would help out with the room because I felt confident I'd be able to finish up the day's editing in a quick burst of activity in the late afternoon. Then a strange thing happened. Lunch was quiet, as usual, but after spooning out my potato salad, my mother pointed at the window behind me. The look on her face was one of puzzlement. Her eyebrows had moved towards each other.

"That ship's been out there for longer than a day," she said. "It hasn't moved."

I turned in my chair. The Japanese ship had looked brilliant and seafaring when Keith and I spotted it yesterday. Today, strangely, the colour of its hull was now a light yellow. Around the ship was a ring of green scum floating on the water.

"It looks abandoned," my mother said.

"Yeah, and you're the expert on ships," I said to my mother.

After she washed the dishes we resumed excavation in the spare room. I had been desperately trying to impose some sort of order in our routine by stacking the photographs, however battered, in one pile, papers that looked official in another pile and newspapers in another. At two-thirty I took a break from the sorting and looked to the water. The freighter was still there, sitting in the middle of the strait. The ring of green scum had widened. It was now close to shore. The seagulls that had been passing above it in thick, cawing, flocks were gone. The whole operation looked to be a bad business venture. I heard the shuffling of papers behind me and turned back to the work at hand, which was the only thing that remained between me and editing the Adventure stories.

"I'll be able to move in properly when this room's clean," I said to my mother.

She looked at me but didn't say anything. I noticed she was taking newspaper clippings off my 'To Be Burnt' pile and reading each one before placing them on smaller piles around the room, which didn't seem to be piles at all. I can't say she pushed them, but suddenly, the stack of *Canadian Living* magazines beside her shifted its weight and slid down towards my head. I put a hand up to catch the fall but it was too late. The magazine stack toppled onto me.

After half an hour on the couch in front of the fire I began to feel marginally better. There was a stack of newspaper clips burning, though it wasn't as big as originally planned. My mother had come in at the last moment and taken a large selection of newspapers back to the room. Beside me was my Ermine notebook, the sort used by Ernest Hemingway and Jonathan Tinders, author of *Management Gain*. I was ready to make editing notes on the first page, but the ship outside held my attention. It still hadn't moved any closer to the harbour but the green foam had reached shore and now spackled the driftwood. "DECEMBER 15, 2003" I wrote in capital letters in my notebook. Then I closed my eyes and began my afternoon nap, accompanied by the hiss of Canadian newspapers in the woodstove.

It was dark when I awoke. The room was faintly illuminated by the yellow floodlights on the ship in the strait, which made it hard to read my editing notes. I took them into the editing suite before realizing the page was blank except for the line "DECEMBER 15, 2003." As I had done enough editing until my evening session, I left for Keith's house. The samurai sword was stuck into the flesh of the arbutus tree out front. Inside Keith was at his telescope. Without moving his eye from the eyepiece he ushered me over and I picked my way through stacks of military books. He was grinning when he turned to me. "Have you seen what this ship is giving off?"

"The green stuff?"

"You know what I found washed up on the shore this afternoon?"

From his fridge he produced the Tupperware container he used for his live bait. Inside was the frothy green foam. Up close it looked like a shaken bottle of Lime Crush.

"Why are you keeping that in the house?" I asked.

"At first I thought it had to be toxic waste," said Keith. "But after it settled I went out—properly protected mind you—and popped open the lid. You know what it did?"

"Turned into algae."

"No. He started talking to me."

I looked at Keith, then down at the Lime Crush foam.

"He?"

"Yeah, this foam actually has a consciousness. Seriously. It talks. He talks. And the weird thing is—and I know this sounds weird—but he's a pretty nice guy. His name's Tim. Didn't say his last name. You want me to open it?"

"Don't open it."

"He's a nice guy. You don't believe me."

Keith put on a pair of Rubbermaid gloves and opened the corner.

"Wait a second," I said. "What does it say to you?"

"He say? Plenty," said Keith. "We talked about outboard engines when I picked him up on the beach. He's a good guy. I think he'll talk to you about anything you want." This time when Keith opened the Tupperware I could hear a mumbling. There was a pause, and then a voice from within the container cleared its throat. "Excuse me."

Keith was already more relaxed. He had propped himself up in the doorway.

"Howdy Tim," he called out.

"Keith buddy. I don't want to drop in on your company."

"You're totally among friends buddy. I should introduce the two of you," he said, moving from the doorway. I swatted my hand down on the lid.

"I don't want to touch it."

"Don't do that. You have to meet him."

"What? Shake his hand?"

"You put your hand out and..." Keith shrugged. "It feels like someone's shaking it." The colour in Keith's face had reddened. "It's just not good manners to interrupt a friend."

"So now he's your best friend?"

"I never said that." Keith opened the container. "But, you know, be polite."

"Oh hello there again," said the deep, male voice coming from the froth. It laughed. "Long time no see."

I felt Keith's hand pushing my arm forward and I gave into it. Something warm enveloped my fingers and held them tightly. I shook and the pressure relaxed."

"That's quite a handshake you've got there," the foam said. "Are you a businessman?"

I ran home. The only lights on were in the spare room and the editing suite. This strange episode had made me ready, I felt, to take on the remaining chapters as soon as I checked in on the progress of the spare room. When I opened the door a woman's voice said: "Keep it." I saw my mother hold up another clipping. "Throw it," the voice said. I closed the door, then knocked a few times. There was a shuffling, then my mother appeared holding a few sheaths of newspaper on top of one of our Tupperware containers. A green foam was sloshing inside. Instead of asking what I'd like for dinner she said "I've got a lot of things to throw out."

I followed her down the corridor.

"What's in the Tupperware?"

"Nothing. I was down on the beach…"

"What were you doing down on the beach?"

"I was having a look at that ship out there."

"Since when are you interested in any ships out there? I point out ships all the time."

My mother set down the container on the table and opened the corner. From it came a small female voice. "You just have to stand up to him, you know. It's not like he has a life of his own, sticking around your house for months at a time." She pressed down the corner.

"So who's this?" I asked. "I've already met Keith's new friend. I suppose this has a name?"

"It's just that…" my mother said quietly. "It's Susan. That's her name. We've had a few good conversations you know."

"Since when?"

"I was down on the beach this afternoon and Susan asked me to pick her up."

"You don't know what this is."

"I asked Susan if she was dangerous," said my mother with finality. "She said no."

"I don't want this in my house," I said.

My mother took the container and set it down on one of the tables she had inherited from my grandmother. "It's not exactly your house, is it?"

She moved the lid off delicately with her fingers, lining up the edges of the container with the photographs on the table. She didn't look me in the eye. "Susan has made me aware of a few things today, a few recent studies of what happens when grown sons return home for an extended length of time."

"Forty-six percent," said the foam.

"Forty-six percent," my mother said louder, "of young men who return home to live with their parents never move out again."

"And fifty-seven percent," said the foam.

"Fifty-seven percent of those young men have unfulfilling relationships and health problems."

"Who told you that?" I asked, perhaps louder than necessary.

"These are facts. These are statistics. And there's one about grown sons who yell at their mothers being susceptible to heart attacks at a young age but I don't know the exact statistic. I'll have to check."

"With your algae."

"With *Susan*."

And she was gone. The glass door to upstairs slammed and rattled. I walked into the editing suite and slammed my own door. I quickly sharpened a red pencil and opened my notebook to edit better than anyone had ever edited before. I sat there. The ship in the strait was still moored. I looked at my hand. Finally, under the date, I began to slowly, methodically practice my signature, alternating those that included my middle name, Claude, with lines of normal Craig Taylors.

Half an hour later, I put the signatures away and looked at my hand again, which was more pale than usual. The warm yellow of the ship's floodlight had gradually changed, turned stark. The lights on the ship were now pulsing. It felt more comfortable to look at them, so I did. Suddenly I didn't want to edit, I wanted to get to the beach to have a better look. When I made it to the waterfront I could see a small pool of what was left of the green foam. The ship's lights continued to pulse, so I sat on a log and watched them until soon my breathing fell in line with their glow.

"It's no easy feat," said a voice nearby. The voice was warm, male, and came, perhaps unsurprisingly, from the small pool of green foam that had collected by the log. The foam bubbled each time it spoke but the voice was clear. "They say business is hard. But editing a book? It's not an easy feat. No walk in the park."

"I'm not listening to you," I said to the foam. I continued to look out at the lights.

"I can't say I blame you," said the foam. "I should be the one listening. Some days I think I know about business, about management. But I'm just a student. You know what I'd love?"

I didn't answer the foam.

"I'll tell you. I'd just love to have someone explain to me how an untested 24 year-old could manage his own McDonald's franchise and make it the most successful on mid-Vancouver Island."

"It was the most successful on *all* of Vancouver Island," I said.

"At twenty-four? It's unbelievable. You know, I look at my own management strategies," said the foam, "and I'd just love to know the secret. I'd love for you to tell me. I know you're a busy guy..."

I stood there silent, eyes on the lights. The foam coughed.

"The secret," I said finally. "is efficiency. And not being afraid of change."

"Not being afraid of change." There was wonderment in the foam's voice. "So true. What about management goals? If you have time to tell me anything else. When I read Jimmy Pattison's book on management..."

"You read *Leadership Secrets*?" I asked.

"Great book," said the foam.

"No, that's not just a great book. That is, like..."

"The Bible."

"I was just going to say the Bible."

"What he says about the quality campaign in '95," said the foam.

"I know, I know."

"Pattison's concept of operational improvement..."

"Was basically mind-blowing," I said. I stood there looking at the foam. I suddenly felt the urge to hold out my hand.

"I'm Craig, by the way." A warm feeling enveloped my fingers.

"Good to meet you finally. I'm Glen. I heard you were looking for some editing help."

The only Tupperware container left in the house was the smallest size, which was fine because there was only about a cup of Glen on the beach. I sat Glen on the desk in the editing suite and spread out the Adventure stories around him.

"A few questions," Glen said when I took the lid off. "Do you have a sharpened red pencil?

"I have five."

"I'd be honoured to edit this thing. It's the least I can do. As friends. And you don't need to stay in the room. I can take care of this."

"There's not any money in this for you," I said.

"There's friendship in it," said the foam slowly, and with weight. "But it's going to be a big job. I'll need a little something from you."

I walked down the hall. The stacks of newspaper outside the spare room were now immaculate. The loose piles of photographs had been replaced by albums with beautiful calligraphy on the front. Before opening the door I listened, and that same woman's voice, Susan's voice, came through the door.

"Sometimes they leave and it's the best possible thing they could do. It's strengthening." Through the crack in the door I saw my mother asleep in a freshly uncovered chair. Around her was carpet and neatness. I slowly opened the door. The voice coming from the Tupperware only had time to say 'Who's that?' before the lid closed.

I stood outside Keith's house, hiding behind the rusting golf cart he had stuck up on blocks. Inside I could see him passing by the blue glare of the TV, returning each time with another element of his evening meal: the pot of beans, the loaf of bread. Finally he went out to the back freezer where he kept his bottles of Moosehead beer. As I got closer I could hear Keith continuing his conversation with the foam from the garage. Tim, in his Tupperware container, was on the counter. Beer bottles clinked from out beyond the screen door. I stepped lightly across the room. "The American's victory in the Pacific," said the foam, "stemmed directly from them choosing to use Saipan as a base. It's like you always say Keith…" and then the Tupperware lid came down.

"Like I always said about what?" Keith called out from beyond the door.

When I poured Susan and Tim into Glen a loud moan came from the mixing bowl. The green foam frothed and thickened before Glen's voice, stronger than before, said: "That certainly makes the job easier." I carried Glen back to the editing suite, set the rest of the stories on the desk in front of him and watched as he worked. The red pencil floated across the page, dipping down occasionally to make marks. When it reached the end, the page lifted up and fluttered to the ground. Glen worked fast, without hesitation. The scene had a rhythm to it and soon I was lulled by the sight of each page lifting and floating to the floor. It all looked good to me. The last thought I had before I fell asleep was whether or not Glen would be interested in starting a company if I offered him the post of Chief Operating Officer. It could be great. There was so much of him in the container now.

The banging on the door woke me. Keith's voice was yelling: "If you've got Tim in there I'm coming in." I quickly turned the light off but the room was still illuminated by the glare of the ship. I grabbed the Tupperware container and the lid. The book, every last story, was immaculately collected on the floor, perfectly edited. "You better come out here," said my mother. "I knew you would start stealing. The instability of living at home and the purposelessness…"

"Don't," said Keith to my mother.

"Never doing the dishes. Never helping with dinner. Now stealing my Susan."

Keith's voice lowered to a whisper. I clicked shut Glen's lid and held my full weight against the door.

"Why don't you just come out and talk to us," said Keith in a far different tone of voice.

"Ask him if Susan's in there," whispered my mother.

"Your mother and I just want to talk to you."

"Ask him."

Keith and my mother were sitting at the table when I came out, empty-handed. Each was holding one of the empty Tupperware containers

I had left in my haste to mix in Susan and Tim. In the middle of the table, near a few green specks of overspill, lay Keith's samurai sword. He had left the case at home.

"If you even lay a hand on Susan," my mother said.

"Mom…"

"Susan has a very sensitive temperament and I promised I would take care of her."

Keith had raised his arms.

"I think we should talk about Tim first."

"Right," I said, "because Tim's your best friend because you've sure known him for so long. He's always ready to go help pick out swords with you."

"At least Tim doesn't always tell me I paid too much because I didn't wait till January."

"January, for your information," I said, "is proven to be the best time to buy non-essential goods. But I guess Tim would know that."

"Could you please tell me where Susan is?" my mother said.

Keith was making eye contact with me. His finger was tapping lightly on the handle of the sword.

"If I waited till January I wouldn't have this now," he said, then pulled the sword towards him.

One of Jimmy Pattison's greatest pieces of management advice is 'Never Taunt.' So I probably shouldn't have said to Keith that I needed the foam, that Glen needed to grow stronger, and that editing this book was far more important than being a friend of a loser who did nothing but write down ships' names all day and couldn't even cook a can of beans properly. I shouldn't have said that he was in love with Tim because he'd never find a woman. I shouldn't have said Tim was a stupid name anyway. Keith looked at me for a long time, then said he needed the bathroom. I guess I should have wondered why he took his sword because as soon as Keith was behind me he stabbed it into my back. My mother let out a small yelp. I said something along the lines of, "What?" We stood there for a moment. Keith gave the sword an extra push and I noticed the blade was now sticking out well past my shirt. "What?" I said again.

"Maybe we should go get Susan," my mother said quietly to Keith. Without acknowledging me again, they walked quickly down the hall to the editing suite, calling out: "Susan are you in there?" and "Tim? Tim?"

Keith grabbed the Tupperware container and ran out the front door. My mother followed quickly, patting his back, not sparing a glance back at me. "Could you hear Susan?" she said. "I'm sure she's in there. I'm sure she's all right." They left the door open until my mother ran back to close it.

I looked down. The blood had begun to spread across my shirt. A tingle was creeping from my chest into my arms. I walked down the hallway. When I entered the editing suite the handle of the samurai sword swung behind me and knocked into the wall, quivering the part of the blade that poked through my chest. I put my hand on it to still the blade and tried to take a deep breath. There was no deep breath. The manuscript of the Adventure book was still perfectly placed on the floor. With some effort I bent down and picked it up, aware of both ends of the samurai sword protruding. I began to read. Glen had done a beautiful job. The finished product was a marvel of editing—never intrusive, never losing sight of the meaning of the story but full of firm and respectful suggestions. Somehow, perhaps because he had no hands, Glen's written notes were all legible and clear. As I had lost feeling in my right hand, I used my left to turn over the final page to read the note Glen had left on the back.

"Well, that should do it partner," it said. "Jeez, it's been good to meet you. I didn't think I'd ever come across anyone who could straddle the worlds of business and literature in such a way. I hope we'll be the best of friends. Can't wait to read this thing in book form! Yours truly, Glen"

From outside I could still hear my mother and Keith calling out for Susan and Tim and sloshing the container around. I closed my eyes and saw an image: Glen and Jimmy Pattison and I were cutting a long red ribbon. The blood was now running down each of my legs. There was blood on my arms. Out in the strait I could still see the mysterious ship. Suddenly, its great floodlights clicked off. Or maybe that was just me closing my eyes. *Craig Taylor*

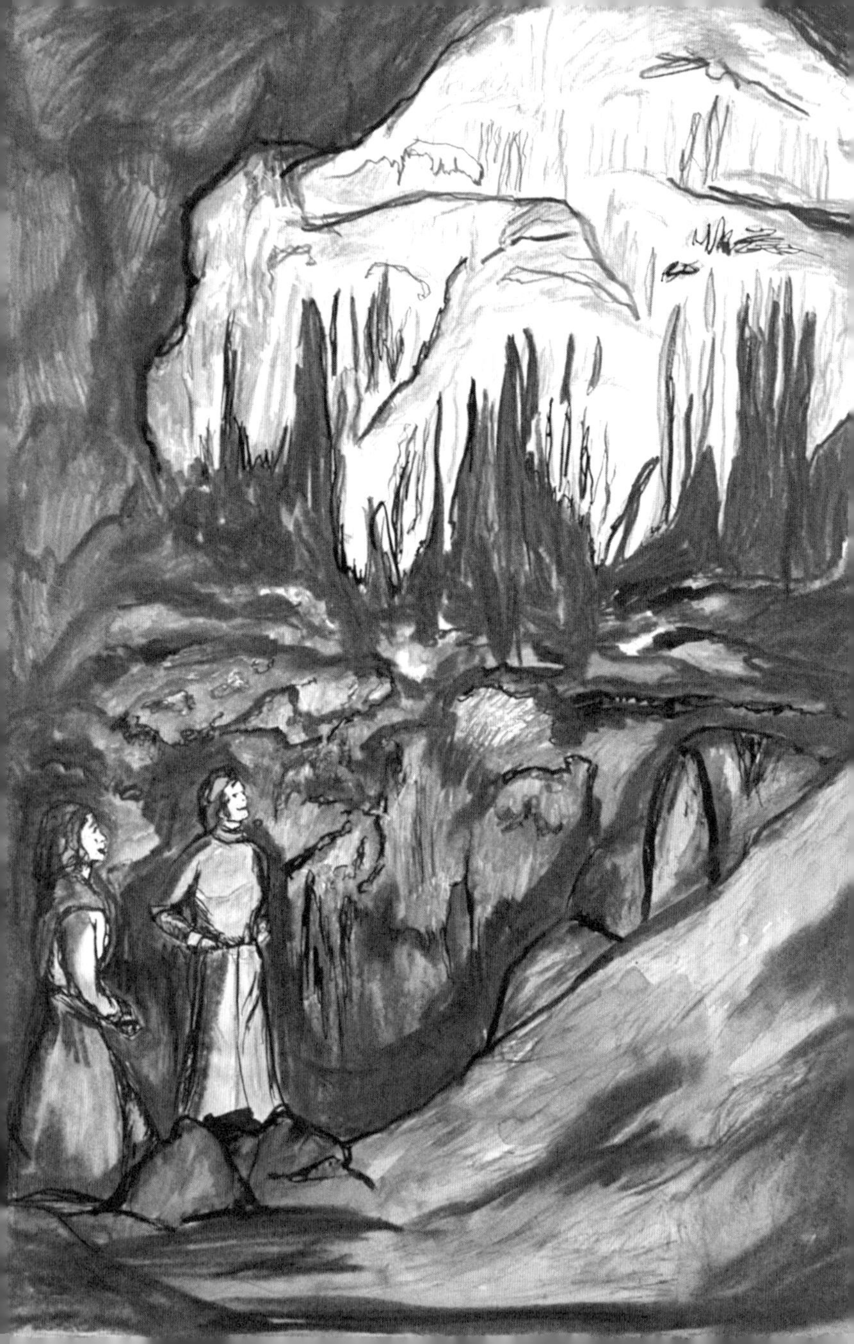

I remember the first time I saw a soldier; I was about six years old, which makes it 1973 or '74. The Nigerian civil war had just ended and the soldiers were returning home from the battlefront—it was late in the evening, one of those long and hot July evenings, and we stood shoulder to shoulder, sweating, by the roadside as the long convoy of trucks with the soldiers in the open back passed through the town center. It was a long convoy, a whole battalion had been stationed to Gombe, our small sleepy town with only one big street running through its center. There were hundreds of us lining the street and waving madly at the trucks that trundled past in the gloom, like a huge worm: the school children screamed, the young women ululated and waved their scarves at the young, dashing soldiers who waved back and raised their guns high in the air.

The next day the soldiers were all around us: in the streets and shops and in the houses, shaking hands, making friends. Some of them sold war mementoes to the

THE NIGHT OF THE MONSTER

by Helon Habila

town's people: bullets, Biafran currency, expired canned food. Tall tales of heroism oiled these transactions and soon the tales passed from mouth to mouth; by the end of the week we could point out which soldier had killed how many people at which battle, suddenly we had war heroes in our midst. That was perhaps why Daniel, my closest friend, said to me, a couple of days later, 'The soldiers are here to kill Hammadu Dangar.'

'How do you know that?' I challenged him. Daniel loved to make up stories to make himself look important. 'They just can't post a whole battalion to Gombe just to kill one man, no matter how dangerous he is.'

'Believe it or not, it is true,' Daniel insisted.

Hammadu Dangar was the most dangerous man in Gombe and the surrounding villages, he was perhaps the most dangerous man alive. He was a bandit, a product of the unsettled, lawless war years. I can't remember when I first heard his name, it seems as if it had always been there on our parents' lips, the bogeyman guaranteed to bring us to order when we became too unruly. He was a myth, a figmental creature who began to gain solidity as the days passed. Suddenly my mother's words began to take on new urgency whenever she did not want me to stay out late.

'Hammadu Dangar loves to cut off little children's ears and make them eat it.'

We kids would regurgitate these stories as we returned home from school in the afternoons, or in the evenings from the football pitch, adding details with each telling, competing with each other to relate the scariest version.

'He has charms that can make him disappear if he wants, that is why he is never caught after robbing his victims,' Daniel, said.

'Last Friday he saw this old woman in the bush, alone. She did not know who he was. He tried to rob her, but she had nothing, no money, nothing. Annoyed, he asked her where she was going to.

"To visit my daughter in the neighboring village, she just gave birth."

"And you came with nothing, no money, no food, not even a loaf of bread to take to your daughter?" he asked angrily. The old woman fell to her knees before him, weeping, begging him not to kill her, because by now he had brought out his long knife and was waving it in her face threateningly.

"No," he said with an evil smile. "I won't kill you. Instead I will give you something to take to your daughter. It is not seemly for you to have come all this way empty handed. What would the neighbors think?"

"Thank you, thank you, may God bless you, young man," the old woman cried. And you know what Hammadu Dangar did next?'

We all knew what he did next, we had heard this story many times before, but we kept quiet, we let the raconteur have his moment. He lowered his voice, his eyes formed two wicked slits as he breathed, 'He cut off her ears and wrapped them all bloody in a cloth and gave them to her. "Give this to your daughter. Tell her from Hammadu Dangar." '

We told the stories in relays, and by the time we got home we'd be so witless with fear that we wouldn't have the courage to go out to play in the night. But of course none of us had ever seen him; all we knew were people who had seen people who had seen him. Some said he was tall, others said he was short but incredibly strong and muscular.

One day I had a chance to talk to a soldier. Late in the evening Daniel had rushed into my room unannounced, breathless, 'Come, come and see! There is a soldier staying in our house,' he gasped. Daniel's house was two blocks away from ours. It was the best house in the neighborhood; his father had just finished building it. It had two garages in the front for their two cars, a huge drug store in the front where the father worked; it was where the whole neighborhood bought its drugs. We entered the house at a dead run, and soon we were standing before Apollo, the soldier, out of breath. He was not as impressive as I had expected. He was seated in front of the storeroom that had been cleared out to accommodate him. The soldiers had to find accommodation where they could because their barracks were still under construction, but most families were happy to take them in. Apollo had moved in the night before, and through the open door behind him we could see a candle burning on a table, it illuminated the room dimly, showing us a tattered canvas bag, still unpacked, lying on the narrow, six springs bed. He was polishing his boots, which he kept raising and peering at, he seemed unsatisfied with his effort even though the boot was already glossy.

'He has to see his reflection in the toecaps before he is done,' Daniel whispered to me. Apollo did not look heroic, he was wearing a green singlet and short knickers—his legs and arms were scrawny, his left jaw was crooked; it had been grazed by a bullet, we later learned. 'If the bullet had gone in an inch more to the right, it would have killed him,' Daniel said.

I stretched out my hand as Daniel proudly introduced me, 'This is my friend, Helon.'

'Ma friend, how you dey?' Apollo drawled. Only one side of his face moved when he spoke, that and his pidgin English, which I was hearing for the first time, made me want to laugh, but something in his, dull, washed out eyes scared me. I ran away.

Apollo became our friend, even after he had moved out of Daniel's house to a room in the brothel across the road we still went to him, and ran errands for him. His favorite haunt was an open zinc shed across the untarred road that passed in front of the brothel where another soldier's wife sold the rot-gut spirit which came to be particularly associated with the soldiers, *Ogogoro*. The soldiers would congregate there in the evenings, some still in their fatigues, knocking back the spirit, playing draughts by lamplight. There were fights there sometimes, and loud war songs, and strong language like

'Fucking bastard' and 'Ah go kill you O!' which gradually found its way into our vocabulary. Apollo was never part of the fights. He always sat to one side, the bored look in his eyes, and for some reason the other soldiers never involved him in their arguments. There were all sorts of stories about him that mostly trickled down to us through Daniel, who was very territorial about Apollo. 'He got that wound in a hand to hand fight with Ojukwu, the Biafran rebel leader,' Daniel would tell us authoritatively, and the next day a new version would emerge, 'He fell from a plane, in a parachute.'

'Pa-ra-chute,' we'd echo, rolling the strange syllables on our tongues.

At this time Hammadu Dangar was in a neighboring town, unleashing mayhem, but the wind of fate was gradually blowing him to our town, and to a fatal meeting with Apollo.

Days, or weeks, or months, after the coming of the soldiers, on a warm evening, the town crier stopped in front of our house and banged on his iron and called out in his loud voice, 'Listen, people of this town, to the words of the king. The king said Hammadu Dangar has been sighted coming to this town. No woman or child should stay out late…'

Daniel and I were thrilled; here at last was our chance to see the monster in the flesh.

Among the adults in our compound the tension was at fever pitch, they tried to hide it from us, but I could see it in my mother's creased forehead as she gazed into the road as if expecting to see something emerge in the distance; and in the hushed conversations that always broke up when a kid appeared. My outings had been reduced to school alone—no more football in the afternoons, or hanging out after dinner with Daniel and other neighborhood kids in front of Daniel's house. I took to spending most of my time in my mother's shop—she was a seamstress with a shop in a long row of shops in front of our house, all the shops faced the narrow strip of tarred road that ran through the town center, and from which smaller dirt roads led to the bar rooms and brothels and cinema halls that lurked in the outskirts of town, 'the devil's quarter' our parents called that part of town. Daily I'd watch the men return from work, dirty and hungry, and a while later come out of their houses in clean shirts and trousers and head off into the alleyways and side streets, to return later in the night, unsteady on their feet, singing songs or cursing, or sometimes all bloody from bar room brawls.

Sometimes prostitutes from the brothel where Apollo lived came to my mother to have dresses made for them. My mother said they paid well.

I'd watch them curiously from where I sat on a wooden bench in a corner. The air would be suffused with their rich perfume; they were always laughing, and talking about their boy friends, and the Indian films they had watched recently. After they had gone I would run my hand on the cloth they had left behind, enjoying its smoothness, imagining it on their skin.

It was on such a day that Hammadu Dangar appeared on our street.

We heard shouts from the first shop in the row, at first we thought it was a fire: it was high-pitched and incoherent with excitement.

'Keep quiet, listen!' my mother shouted at her chattering apprentices, Jummai and Ladi.

'Hammadu Dangar! Lock your shops!' the words were clear now.

Hammadu Dangar! My mother was like a mother hen whose chicks are threatened by a hovering falcon. 'Grab everything you can and get into the shop, now!' she screeched at us. She pushed her chair back and got out from behind her sewing machine, grabbing the cloth basket off the cutting table. Now we could hear other shops slamming shut as the words of warning reached them. My mother grabbed my arm and pulled me after her, in a minute we were inside the tiny shop, the door firmly closed behind us.

I could hardly breathe; I was slowly asphyxiating from tension within me and the pressure of women's bodies pressing into me from all sides. My mother was peeping out through the keyhole. 'Can you see him?' I whispered.

'SSSH!' the women hissed at me.

Then miraculously I found my right eye staring out into the street—a nail hole had magically appeared in the door at my eye level. Then I saw him. I had no doubt it was him even though I had never seen him before. He was standing in the middle of the deserted street—he was tall and resplendent in a big, ankle-length robe, on his head was a thick white turban. He was too far away for me to see his face clearly, but his carriage was arrogant, his face haughty. He looked up and down the long, empty street. When he moved there was a slight stagger to his steps. He was obviously from the devil's quarter. Then he was gone. After a long while the street began to stir back to life. The monster had passed.

That was the evening he met Apollo in a bar room, the night he died.

The whole town came out to see the fight, and to view the dead body, which lay in a ditch for two days afterwards, but I did not see it. For the two days that the excitement lasted I was forbidden to go out by my parents, I was like a dog on a leash, restless, resentful, but helpless.

'For two days he lay in the ditch, that gully that runs alongside the path we take to school,' Daniel told me. He had seen it all. The gully ran the length of the devil's quarter, the rowdiest, raunchiest section of town, and often on our way to school early in the mornings we'd see evidences of what took place the night before: a drunk still curled up on the steps before a bar room, a prostitute throwing out a tardy customer, her wig askew, the make up streaking down her face. And broken bottles of beer all over the road.

The fight had started in one of the bar rooms.

'Moonshine Hotel,' Daniel said.

Night had almost fallen when Hammadu Dangar staggered into the ill lit bar room, his cruel eyes bleary, he had two giggly girls clinging to his arms. A hush descended on the room as soon as people recognized him, some slinked away through the rear exit, abandoning their drinks. Others too drunk to make a quick exit shrank into their seats, averting their faces whenever Hammadu Dangar glanced their way. Only Apollo sat in his corner, his head buried in his glass, oblivious to what was going on. He had been in that posture all evening, not drinking much, just seated alone and silent.

'The fight began when one of the girls went over to Apollo and asked for a light,' Daniel said, 'but other people said that Hammadu Dangar asked Apollo for a drink and Apollo refused him.'

I could imagine the girl, thin and giggly, her face crusty with make up, her eyes shiny from too much drink, crossing the room to where Apollo sat, his cigarette just lighted. She sat down at his table for a moment after getting the light; she might have let her hand linger too long over his as she returned the box of matches. Or perhaps, when she got back to Hammadu Dangar she said, 'That man said we are making too much noise. Perhaps he doesn't know who you are.' Her eyes glittered with malicious expectation as Hammadu Dangar staggered to his feet, his face contorted with rage. He knocked down chairs and tables in his way as he made for Apollo's table; he was like a tidal wave, a tornado on the move. Apollo did not look up when Hammadu

Dangar towered above him and banged his hand loudly on the table, making the beer glass fall and roll off the table, pouring drink into Apollo's lap.

'What do you want?' Apollo asked. His eyes were sunken deep in his gaunt face; his private demons had him on the rack, torturing him mercilessly.

'My name is Hammadu Dangar,' the bandit thundered, for he could see that this man had not recognised him.

'What do you want?' Apollo repeated dully, his words distorted by his crooked mouth.

'I want you out of here. I want you to apologize to my girlfriend. No, I think I am going to kill you,'

Hammadu Dangar said, the big white turban on his head made him look bigger, taller. Slowly, deliberately, he reached under his robe and brought out a broad bladed butcher's knife, and smiling, held it on the table before Apollo.

'People said it was at this point that Apollo suddenly came to life,' Daniel said, 'He gave a laugh that was even scarier than the bandit's. His hand shot out and grabbed Hammadu Dangar's knife hand at the wrist.'

Hammadu Dangar felt the strength in that grip; it forced his fingers to open, to drop the knife. Apollo's eyes glittered feverishly, and in their depths Hammadu Dangar saw a madness threatening to break its bounds.

'Leave me alone,' Apollo said through his crooked mouth. He stood up slowly and stared deep into the bandit's eyes, then he released the hand and left the room. But Apollo did not go home from there, he went to another bar room and ordered a beer, which he took to a corner, just like in the other bar, and lowered his face over his glass. About an hour later Hammadu Dangar came in, this time there was only one girl with him, the thin, malicious one. He was very drunk, he had been looking for Apollo from bar to bar, hurling insults in the streets, knocking down anyone that stood in his way. And now at last he saw him, sitting in the corner, hunched over his drink, not talking to anyone. He went straight to Apollo's table…

'That was where the real fight began,' Daniel said. 'It was to last for hours, it extended from bar room to bar room, into the streets and ditches, even into people's houses.'

Soon Apollo was all bloody from stab wounds, but he wouldn't give up. Hammadu Dangar could not be cut by knife, or bottle. He had medicine that turned metal into water, and glass into sand, on contact with his skin. But Apollo would not give up. They fought from early evening till late into the hot, starless night; they tumbled in the sand and into the open gutters. Both were down to their shorts—Apollo's body was thin and tough, like raw hide, like wire, Hammadu Dangar was fat and muscular, round his arms and waist dangled assortments of charms, some looked like infants' skulls.

Soon the word spread all over town: a crazy soldier was fighting Hammadu Dangar. The devil's quarter filled up with people following the fighters from the bar rooms to the narrow alleys, they cheered Apollo, urging him on, even though it was clear that he could hardly stand on his feet. But he wouldn't quit. Then suddenly, when Hammadu Dangar had knocked Apollo down and was standing over him, swaying from side to side, chanting self praises, a stone whizzed out of the gloom and connected with his face. A gash appeared below his left eye, he held his face, blood spurted between his fingers, the people cheered.

'Kill him,' the crowd screamed. 'Stone him to death,' the people shouted. Now the crowd took over from where Apollo had stopped. Stones whizzed out of the dark, connecting with dull thuds to the bandit's body. Soon he was reeling about, his hands covering his bleeding face. The crowd screamed and roared.

'Then the bandit gave a loud roar and charged at the crowd. The people turned and took to their heels, popping out of the narrow streets like rabbits from their holes, and whenever the bandit stopped they also stopped and threw stones at him,' Daniel said, 'I was there. You should have seen his bloody face, the blood dripping down his big hands and shoulders.'

'And where was Apollo at that time?' I asked.

'Still down, forgotten in the melee. Finally the crowd chased the bandit into the gully, throwing stones at him till he died.'

Apollo became something of a town hero after that day. People stopped him on the streets to shake his hand, people bought him drink in the bar rooms, then one day his battalion was transferred to another town and nothing was heard of him again.

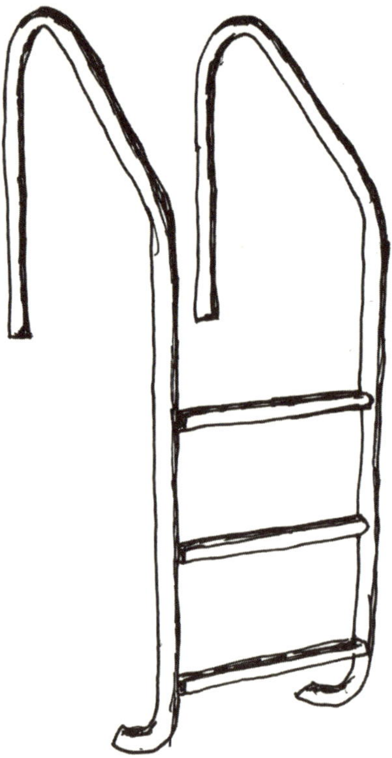

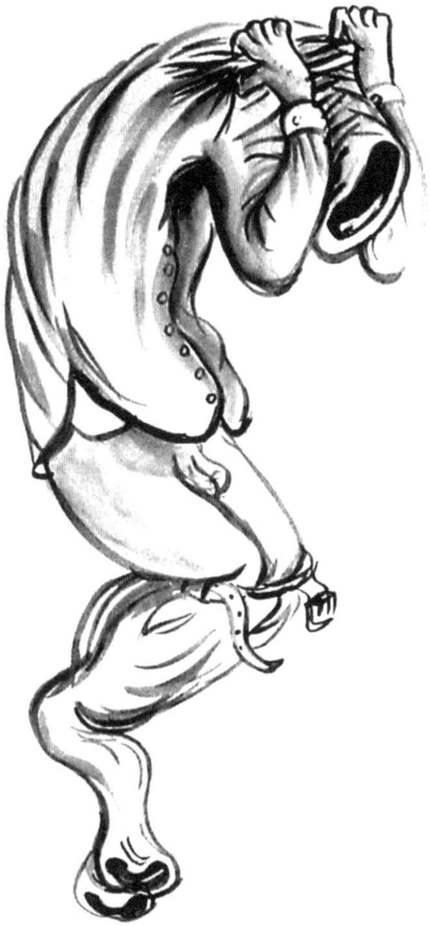

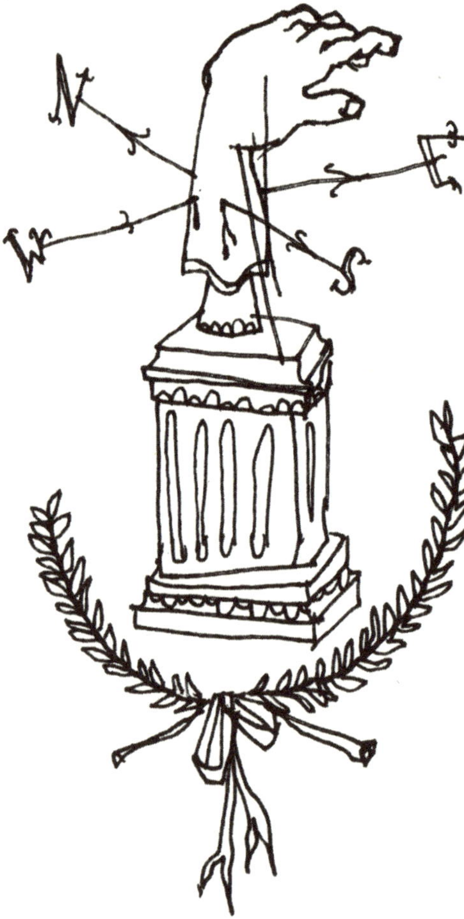
N
E
W
S

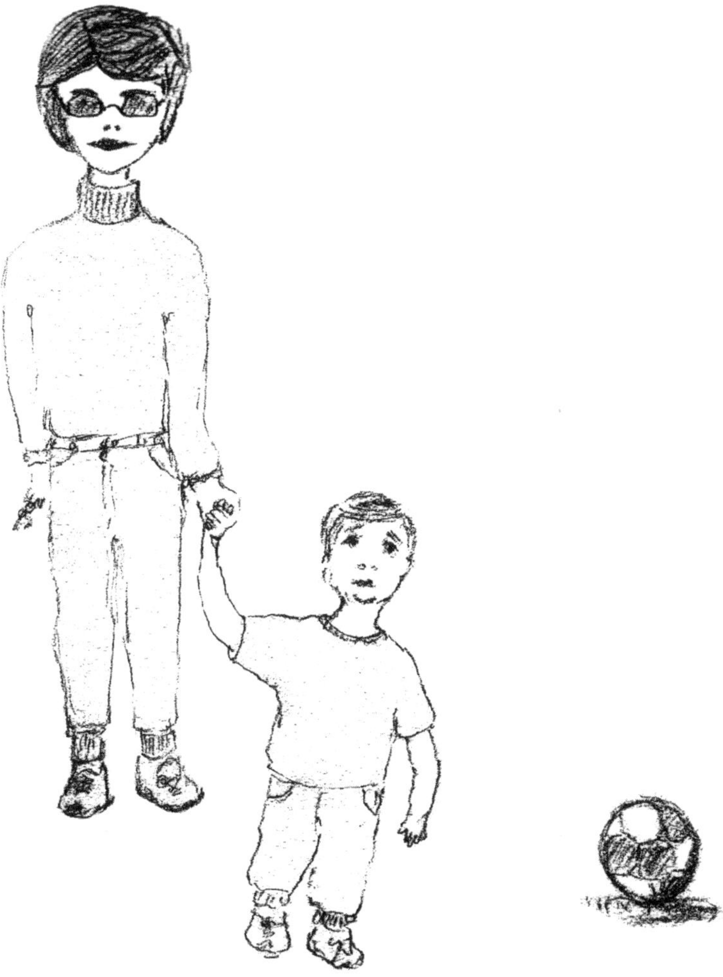

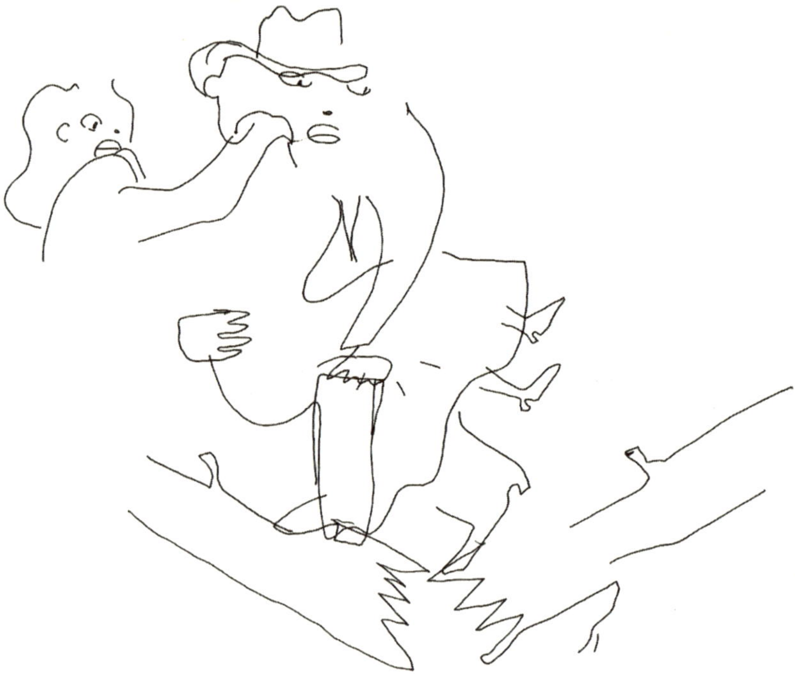

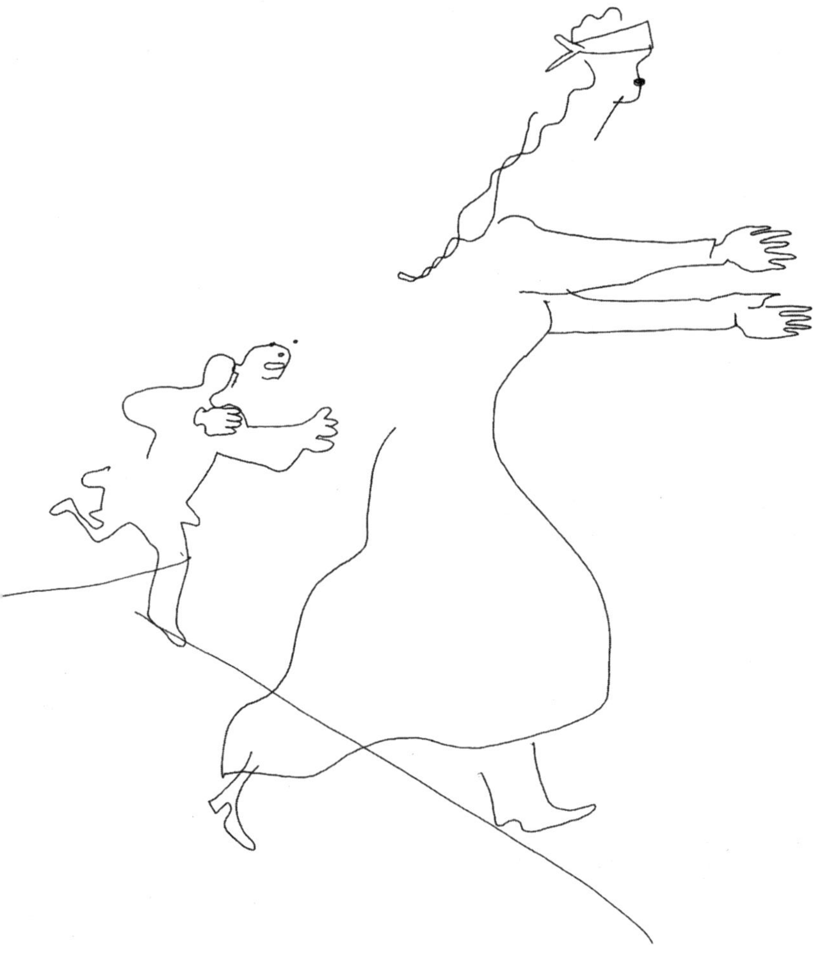

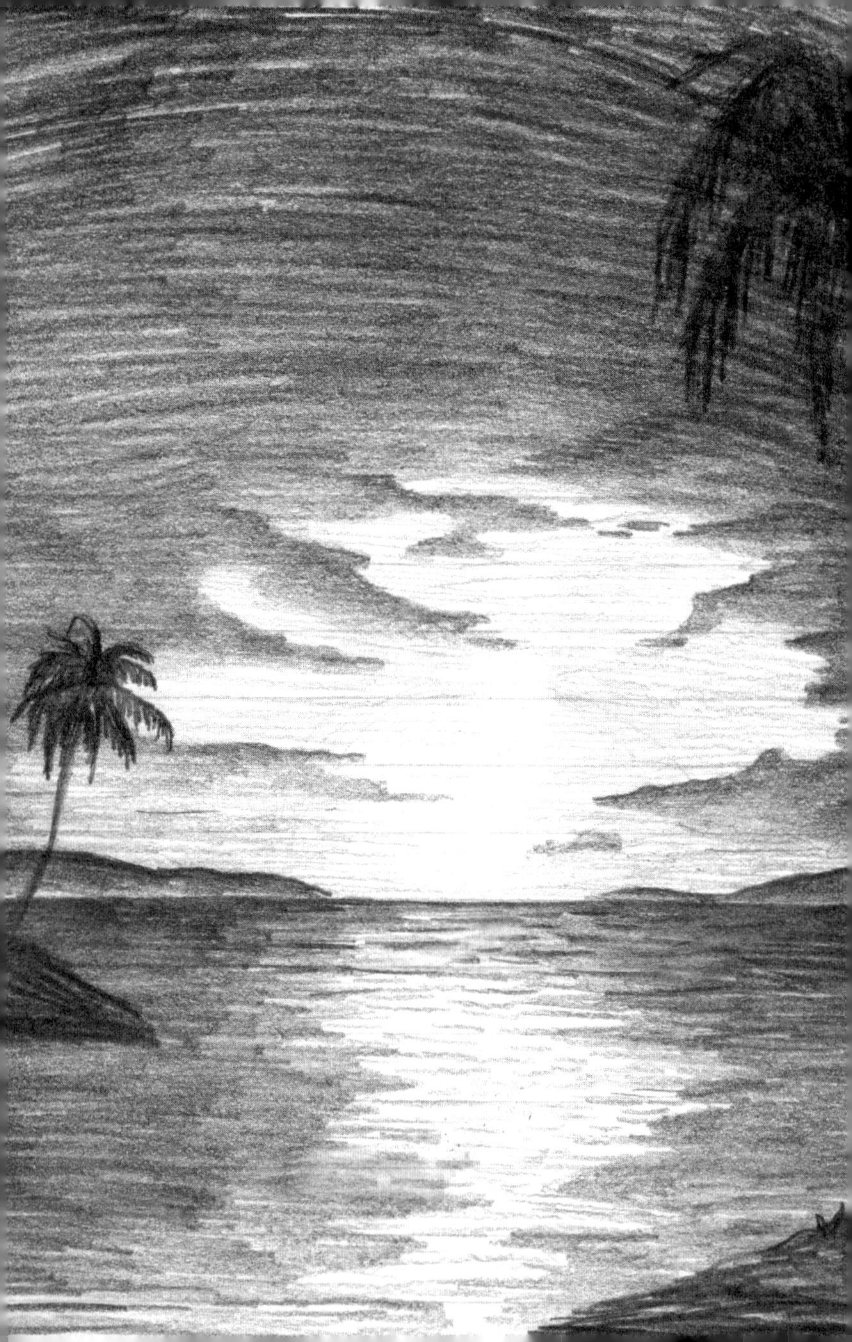

Carol Loewen and I are thirty-eight years old and we've been best friends since we were ten. "Best friends" is a kind of childish expression but we don't care. These days we sit around a lot and talk about our kids and our jobs and how cold it is outside and how hateful Revenue Canada is and how we should have wills by now and how tired we are and how the biggest thrill is when Clinique Bonus time rolls around and we can buy our dramatically different moisturizer and get a gift make-up bag of stuff like Heather Moon lipstick or a Happy perfume sample.

We were sitting in the Bar Italia a couple of Sundays ago—our husbands play hockey together on Thursday evenings and Carol and I shoot pool and drink wine together on Sunday afternoons—talking kind of languidly about things like shoulder fat and water wings and how maybe it's time to quit our jobs or learn another language or pack up the family and sail around the world or something, anything different, just one big change before it's too late, when all of a sudden we heard a few bars of this song that was huge in the hot,

ALL OVER

by Miriam Toews

hot summer of 1980 when we were sixteen and growing up in the small prairie town of Steinbach, Manitoba. I wanna kiss you all over and over again… 'til the night closes in. I don't know what it's called or who the band is or the singer or anything but it's a very sexy song. At least it seemed that way to us back then. So as soon as we heard that song in the bar we almost simultaneously said to each other oh my god remember the Morris Stampede and magically our words started speeding up and we were saying I know, I know, and then, and then, things like that, as though we had woken up refreshed from a long, deep nap.

We had just turned sixteen and gotten our drivers licenses and it was really hot outside, early July, and we needed somewhere to drive to and something to do—we had both kind of forgotten that we were supposed to be painting this giant dairy barn but I'll get to that later—and so we just thought hey, yeah, the rodeo in Morris, rides, cowboys, let's go! Morris was another small town on the other side of the river about thirty miles away, really close to the American border. We found it on a map that was in the glove compartment of my dad's huge Custom 500 Ford. We had all the windows open and the radio cranked and Carol was screaming while she tried to keep the map from blowing out the window and I was screaming do I turn here? Do I turn here? We both wore almost exactly the same thing: skin tight Fancy Ass jeans with bolts on the sides, ropy Jesus sandals, our bikini bathing suit tops, feathered hair, mine blonde, hers brown, combs in our back pockets, chocolate mint lip gloss, heavy eye-liner, blue eye shadow, and Love's baby soft perfume. Am I burning? we'd ask each other periodically as we walked around the fairgrounds. Comb, one of us would say and then we'd pass the comb back and forth and just stop wherever we were, and flip our hair around, bending at the waist, throwing back our heads, huge process, and then keep walking. I think our main goal was basically to walk around and be lusted after by the midway boys. Have them nod, in a barely perceptible but *intense* kind of way when we pass, feel their eyes burning holes into our bare backs and feathered hair as we disappear. Have them leer at us and growl, with cigarettes dangling from the corners of their mouths, so you wanna go faster? Yeah? I can't hear you. Did you say you wanna go faster? Well, then, lemme hear you screeeeeaaaam. That was all and it was everything. But after a bit of that we decided to go look at the horses. We were walking through this barn, it was dimly lit and really hot and smelled like ammonia, and we could hear a radio playing softly and some guys with American accents talking and laughing. We passed by some giant soulful looking horses and then, at the other end, we saw the American guys in a big stall with two horses that they were washing and they were just kind of fooling around with the water and soap, throwing it at each other, slopping it around. They were around our age, maybe a year or two older, and they wore

Wranglers and cowboy boots, obviously, and really, really white t-shirts with the sleeves cut off. We hung out with these guys, they were real cowboys, bronc busters, from Wyoming, and I think their names were Clay and Tyson but maybe I'm just imagining that. They talked to us first, asked us if we were lost, if we liked horses, what our names were, how old we were, all that, they put their cowboy hats on us and introduced us to their horses, pretended to spray us with their hoses, us screaming no, don't, no, don't and then we listened to them talk in a kind of laughing way with their beautiful Wyoming cowboy language and watched them wash their horses and get them ready for their big event that was going to happen later that evening. They hauled out this bale for me and Carol to sit on and even put this saddle blanket over it so we wouldn't get poked with straw and then they rolled a joint which we all passed around and when we started coughing they put their thumbs over the end of the hose so the water came out gently in a trickle and we all had a drink. Clay or maybe it was Tyson started going on and on about ropin'. How if he had his way he'd be ropin' all day, how he just lives for ropin'. What do you ladies live for? he asked us. We said we didn't know, nothing really. C'mon, they said, you have to live for something and we kept saying nope, we don't. Then they started talking about how it could be nice for the four of us to hook up later on, after their event, maybe check out this party they'd heard about at some dam and Carol and I just laughed like we knew they were going to get around to that question, we were so confident, and we said yeah, maybe, hmmm, and watched them lather up their horses and rinse them off with warm water and brush them and run their big square hands over them and comb their tails and their manes in a real gentle, loving and erotic way. It was so hot in that barn and the pot they'd shared with us had been really strong and their shirts were so blindingly white and their voices so smooth and weird and everything seemed to be happening in slo-mo and everything Carol and I said was funny and smart, or it seemed that way to us, even if we couldn't think of anything really to live for like roping, and Clay and Tyson were telling us they'd been on the road for weeks and it was nice to talk to girls who smelled good, what was that smell they asked, and we were hot and the night was long and life was short and it was just a natural thing that we should hook up later and they'd smile and look away and so would we and then that song started to play on the radio I wanna kiss you all over and over again and I think we were all dying, all four of us, wanting to know what was going to happen next, and then . . . nothing did. Some old guy, one of their dad's, came along and told them to haul ass out to some other part of the barn, and Carol and I got up off the bale, said we had to leave anyway, took their cowboy hats off, handed them back to Clay and Tyson, and said Goodbye. I also remember adding "and good luck in your event later tonight" and Clay or maybe it was Tyson said in this really sombre voice, "thank you kindly ma'am", and we walked away and they watched us walk away for a few seconds until the old guy said Let's go, boys, move.

On the way home Carol and I were quiet and the wind had died down and it was pitch black and comfortably warm and we watched bugs swirl around in the headlight beams. The car windows were still open and our hair was still perfect and we weren't tired at all and we suddenly remembered that we had forgotten about our painting job so we drove straight down this little gravel road to Curtis's hip-roofed barn and worked all night in our bathing suits so we wouldn't get our clothes covered in paint. We were perched way up high on scaffolding made from boards and tires and then Ed, the farmhand who wanted to date "either one of us", came and parked his Red Phantom, a souped up Camaro, right beside the scaffolding and told us he'd heard our car on the gravel (What? we asked him. What? We always said what to Ed) and he opened up his trunk where he had installed speakers and turned on the radio, softly, so Curtis and his wife and kids wouldn't wake up in their house across the yard, and after a while we heard that same song playing yet again and Carol and I did a groovy, sort of stupid little dance way up on the scaffolding, under the giant yellow yard light, for Ed who was standing on the ground and staring up at us grinning. It was the summer of I want to kiss you all over and over again. The part about 'til the night closes in sounded tragic to us, like the guy was on the run or something.

But the thing that we loved best about the song and would never have been able to articulate at the time was that the guy was singing about *wanting* to kiss the girl all over and over and it was all about pure desire and that was just our speed back then, we didn't need anything more complicated than that, all we needed was to know that anything was possible. And then, just as the sun was beginning to come up, Carol and I decided to call it a day and we threw down our empty paint cans to Ed who caught each one and then we climbed down fearlessly from the fifty foot scaffolding with our scrapers between our teeth and our brushes in the waistbands of our bikini bottoms, jumped the last five feet, bummed a couple of smokes off Ed, thanked him for the tunes and then hosed the paint off our bodies with purple gas from the big tank behind the barn.

Yeah, we said, me and Carol, sitting in the Bar Italia, remembering that night, shaking our heads. We were so bold, I said. We didn't even care, said Carol. We had no idea. We thought it would always be that simple. I know, I said. Like all we had to do was show up. Like we'd just snap our fingers. I know, said Carol, but it's not like we're that old. No, I said. Look at Frances McDormand. She's still really sexy and she's even older than us. Yeah, said Carol, but the thing is she's Frances McDormand. Yeah, that was true. But there was something else that Carol and I were remembering, something other than sexiness, something more like the opposite of sexiness maybe, we weren't entirely sure, and we didn't have the time to figure it out. After drinking the last of our wine we paid the young hipster guy behind the counter and went home to our husbands and kids. We're relatively sure that our husbands still desire us, it's not like we're obsessed with aging or anything like that, it was just that damn song that set us off. Normally Carol and I rarely, if ever, talk about that day. To tell you the truth that day at the Morris Stampede and the night painting and all that stuff didn't seem at all like a huge adventure at the time—it was pretty standard material in a prairie girl's life. It's only looking back at it, remembering how unbelievably confident we were, and how we carried ourselves in a world we truly thought we *owned*, that makes it seem now like some kind of epic tale, like we were movie stars or something in our own lives, like who the hell *were* those kids?

After we'd finished painting we went home except for one more stop at the Blumenort gravel pits for a swim and to rinse the purple gas off our bodies and we watched, as we floated around like starfish on our backs, the little rainbow pools of gasoline explode into flames when we lit them with our Bic lighters and then just as quickly fizzle out and die. And the sun was coming up and we knew our parents would be getting up soon and if we weren't in our beds they'd panic and get upset so we got out of the water and into the car and drove to Carol's place and while we were driving those one or two miles through shimmery blue fields of alfalfa and other stuff that grew we wondered what the odds were of us hearing that song on the radio one more time that night and so we flipped around from station to station and then just as we were turning the corner onto Henry Street where she lived it came on, I think it was CFRW, and we sat in her driveway and listened to the whole song all over again with our heads back and our feet up on the dash and our arms stretched out across the top of the seat breathing in the sweet summer air of yet another perfect day and knowing, yup, we were the girls who called the shots, the girls who lived to live. Well, maybe we were thinking that. I can't honestly remember. We might have been thinking of Clay and Tyson or Ed or the midway boys and how it would feel to have any one of them kissing us all over til the night closed in or maybe in some weird unspoken barely sixteen year old and completely unacknowledged way, we were revelling in our innocence, soaking it up, storing it in our bodies and memories, filling every empty container in the house, in anticipation.

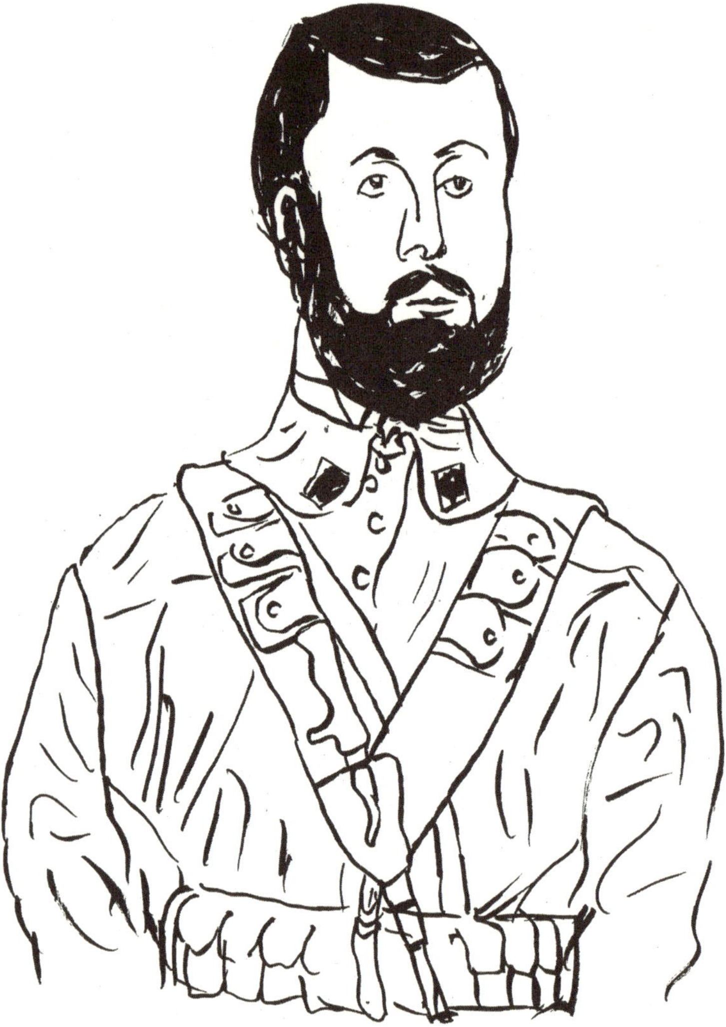

LADIES!

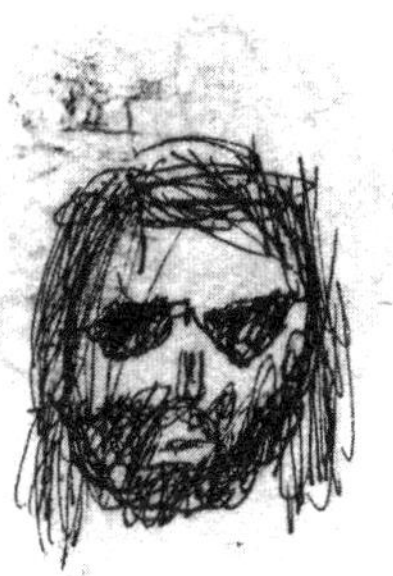

DO NOT

GO TRAIPSING

ACROSS THE

LAND FOR

THIS MAN

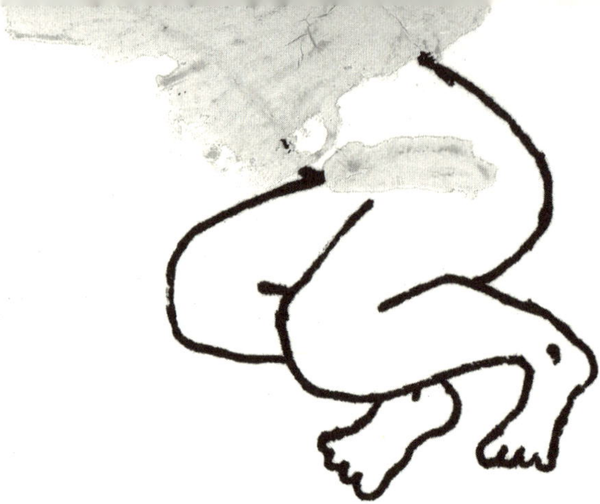

The number four most requested song began playing. Conner had three and a half minutes to talk on the phone. "When does she have to go back to the doctor?" he asked.

"Next Monday," she said. "That'll be your day. Plus I'll need your half for daycare. So you owe me three hundred and sixty dollars now."

"Okay. I'll get it to you by next Wednesday when I drop her off."

Conner pressed the button on the switchboard and his ex-wife's voice ceased in his head. He turned up the sound in his headphones and tried to nudge himself into some sort of rhythm that would shake his mind from his troubles. He often found that if he let his body swell with the music while he worked his night shift, the problems in his head subsided or at least were clouded over momentarily. He called the weather line quickly to get the current numbers before the song faded out. He popped in the weather bumper and hit the button that triggered its dramatic intro: Portland-Portland w-w-w-w-weather!

"Fifty-eight degrees on a sweet Thursday night. Expect it to be a little cooler tomorrow, with a high around sixty-six. You keep asking for it, we keep giving it

KRYSTAL

by Kevin Sampsell

to ya', here's the newest from Ricky Martin; the third-most requested on the Killer, KKLR." He had three minutes and sixteen seconds. He answered phones.

Conner wasn't surprised anymore about the immaturity of his audience. They had thin, frail voices like rubber squeak toys and could barely pronounce the word "request." Once in a while he would get into these awkward conversations with lonely teen-age girls. These were his radio groupies.

They were girls barricaded in their houses by their controlling parents. Girls who found it easier to talk on the phone or send e-mails rather than talk with people face-to-face, body-to-body, insecurity to insecurity.

"You've called the Killer."

"Can I ask you something?"

"Sure. Whaddaya want to hear?"

"What?"

"What song would you like me to play."

"No. I mean, I just wanted to ask you if you knew something."

"Okay. What is it?"

"Is Ricky Martin gay?" The voice belonged to what sounded like a 13-year-old white girl trying to sound black. Conner turned to look at one of the posters of the Latin pop star that hung throughout the station.

"Well, he does wear leather pants that lace up in the front. That's serves as a clue for me."

"So, will you guys stop playing him if he turns out gay?"

"No. I don't think that's a factor anymore. Ever hear

of Elton John?"

"Who?"

"Never mind."

"Are you gay or something?"

"No. Sorry to let you down."

"My dad says that Conner Cavanaugh sounds like a gay name."

Conner sucked a strawfull of Mountain Dew in his mouth and let the taste seep into his tongue. "I think some uncles on my dad's side of the family leaned that way but their name was Litswick."

"Huh?"

"Did you want to request a song?"

"Do you have a girlfriend?" Her sentence seemed to be punctuated by a drag on a cigarette.

"No. I'm too young," he lied.

"Yeah, right. I bet you're like forty years old and married."

Conner twisted in his chair, putting things that looked like old eight-track tapes into the machines around him. He pushed a button and an electronic voice said, "Portland's non-stop music station. The K-K-K-K-Killer." The second most requested song started with no music, just vocals. Some country music singer doing the cross-over into pop.

"I hate this guy," the girl on the phone said. "All those country music people are racists."

Conner thought about responding to that but learned from previous experience that it was useless to argue with a teenager. "So, what's your name?" he asked.

"Why, are you going to ask me out on a date?"

"No. No, no, no."

"You're not going to ask me out?"

Conner tried to think of something clever to say, something that would leave that option open. She did sound kind of cute. He let out a short noncommittal huff.

"Well, my name is Kristy, but my friends call me Krystal."

Conner wrote her name down so he wouldn't forget. He thought of Crystal Methamphetamine. He had never done it before because he thought it would probably make him delusional. He saw television news shows that talked about people who thought they could fly or people who could be hit in the face with a hammer and not feel it because they were on the drug. *Did he just see that on TV?* Maybe he saw that when he was a kid. They were more freaked out by drugs when he was a kid.

"So, where are you calling from, Krystal?"

"Southeast. Out by Oregon City. Where do you live?" It had come out so quick, so smooth that it caught Conner a little by surprise. Was she making a move?

"I live out that way too. In that area around 82nd. All those used cars."

"You ever go to that paintball place. The Battlezone?" she asked him.

Paintball. He'd thought about playing it when it first became popular but none of his friends wanted to. Who played paintball anyhow? Teenagers? War veterans?

Jocks? Lawyers? Was it cool?

He cleared his throat. "I haven't been there before. Do you go there?" he asked.

"I've only done it once but I go there sometimes with my brother and just play the video games."

"Only played once, huh?"

"Yeah, it's such a jock thing. These guys were shooting at my tits."

"Nice." He immediately felt weird saying that. He realized he had to get ready for the next song. "Hey, hold on a second, okay?"

He pushed a button and brought up his mic volume. "Here it is. For the third night in a row. The most requested song on the Killer." A glassy computerized drum beat pounded and a pair of rappers began to rap so fast over the beat it almost made the need for it unnecessary. Conner could barely understand every other word. Slang slang slang beep/slang slang slang beep beep…

"I love this song," Krystal said when he punched her line back up.

"Yeah, well. There's actually a couple of other songs on their CD that are a lot better," he said. *Was he sounding too snobby for her?* "I mean, yeah. It's a cool song though."

It sounded like she laughed a little, or sighed, or yawned. "Do you want to meet me at the Battlezone this weekend? I mean, I'm going to be there, like, with a couple of friends and stuff. They would think it's cool to meet you."

He lingered near the change machine with a couple

of crisp one dollar bills in his hand. It was just past two in the afternoon and the place was crowded. He had no idea how he would tell her from the others. He saw a couple of girls that he wished were her but knew they probably weren't. She told him that she looked a little like Julia Roberts but she was half-Mexican and not as skinny. That could have meant anything. Sometimes he looked in the mirror and saw Sean Penn looking back. Or Sean Penn's chubbier older brother. It depended on his mood.

One girl came up and asked him for a cigarette. He didn't want to give her one but he did anyway, just to try and talk with her. "Do you know a girl named Krystal?" he asked nervously.

"Oh sure," she said, snapping her gum and lighting her free Marlboro. "Go over to the bathroom and pretend you're watching the battles on the TVs."

He was going to question her but he already felt stupid. He was probably getting involved with another high school freshman. He watched the girl as she weaved through the kids, supposedly to find Krystal.

There was a big monitor near the bathrooms so anyone could watch some of the paintball battles going on in the other part of the huge old building. The screen was divided into four sections and he watched a variety of wild-eyed cavemen slumping through and sometimes little kids as well, paint splattered and limping with grimaces on their faces. He looked for any females doing battle but had no luck. He painfully felt the need to see a woman with paint splattered on her chest.

"You want Crystal?" a young man next to him said. Conner looked over and saw a tall teenager wearing a mesh T-shirt and baggy jeans. The young man had a buzz-cut and his hands dug so deep and recklessly in his pants that Conner could see his pubic hair poking out, red and gangly. Pushed down any further, the kid's dick would come flopping out.

"I was just supposed to meet Krystal and some of her friends," Conner informed him.

"Friends, huh?"

"Yeah, um… do you know the Krystal I'm talking about? Looks kind of like Julia Roberts but a little heavier. Part Mexican."

The teenager laughed viciously, his pants almost falling. "C'mon," he said, and held the door to the bathroom open. No one else was in there. "Here," he said undoing the loose belt on his pants. "This ain't really Mexican but that shit is so bogus anyway. If you want some real imported stuff you should try Canadian." Conner watched as the teenager pulled a bag of powder from the inside of his pants. In the dull bathroom light it looked gray and sand-like. Conner felt his arm move without him. He grabbed the bag and sensed its weight.

The door swung open and an older man lunged in. He was wearing a white battle suit and it was covered in orange and green paint. "God damn, they got me in the ear! Fucking hearing aid's all fucked. God damn!" The teenager grabbed the two dollar bills out of Conner's hand and darted from the bathroom before the door even closed behind the wounded man. Conner stuffed the bag in his jacket and headed out as well. "Hey! A little help, God damn you! Can I get a little help?!" the splattered man called out.

Conner made his way back to the change machine and looked for the girl he had given the cigarette to. He wasn't quite sure what just happened in the bathroom. Was he daydreaming? He thought that since he had to pay so much attention to everything at work that sometimes he spaced off when he was out doing other things. Once, he took his daughter to the park to play and as he sat on a bench, his little girl, then three years old, wandered too close to the skateboarders and accidentally got hit. Her arm was broken and she had to wear a tiny pink cast for three weeks.

"Hey, are you the DJ?"

Conner looked at a young girl whose resemblance to Julia Roberts was nowhere to be found. "Hey. Krystal?" he asked.

"I can't deal with this place anymore. Let's go for a ride or something."

As they walked outside, Conner felt a nervous surge heating up around his armpits. She looked like she could be eighteen and she was actually pretty attractive. Like Rosanna Arquette in *Desperately Seeking Susan*. He felt a pliable energy around her, as if he could eventually have his way with her, sooner not later.

Conner held the door of his Rabbit open for her. He started it up and the squall of an old hard rock song slipped out of his stereo until he turned it down. As they were pulling out of the parking lot, the tall teenage boy who had given him the bag in the bathroom came rushing up to his window. "Hey buddy. Hey. Hey!" Conner pulled out into traffic and tried to pretend he didn't know the kid. He turned up the radio again but could still hear the yelling. "You only gave me two dollars!"

"I know who that guy was," she kept saying as they drove. Conner was going to take her to his apartment but he was driving in a strange roundabout pattern, hoping she would not remember how to get to his place. She kept jabbing him and smiling weirdly, like they'd known each other for a long time and she knew when he was hiding something. "I know you got something from that guy," she said.

"I don't know who that guy is. You tell me," Conner finally said, trying not to smile too much.

"Let me see what you got from him."

Conner pulled out the bag and placed it gently in her lap. He tried to gauge her reaction. "Pull over right here," she said anxiously. They pulled up next to a closed barber shop. "This looks like the same stuff I had last weekend. Good fuckin' shit."

Conner didn't want to ask what it was. He was cool enough to have it, wasn't he? Why blow his cover now? He thought for a few seconds that maybe he should become more of a druggie. Especially if it meant getting to mess around with Arquette-look-a-likes and watching old army vets have their hearing aids blasted out by paintball psychos. She pulled out a popsicle stick and wet it with her tongue. She brought up a perfect mountain-shaped lump and snorted it up her flexing nostril. She licked the rest off and passed the stick to me. *What happened to using straws?*

He looked around quickly and then took a little onto his tongue. It tasted like shit. "Snort it," she said. He hadn't snorted anything before. He tried a smaller mountain for his nostril but exhaled as he brought it up and it blew off, falling dust-like onto his pants. She smiled a little and her eyes looked red. "Out of practice?" she said playfully. Conner looked down at his pants and started to brush it off. "No, wait," she said. She leaned over and put her face near his lap. She sucked it up gently, little snoring sounds escaping the back of her throat. She sat up straight then and tilted her head back a little. "Clean pants," she said.

As he was finally pulling up to his apartment building, she started to seem nervous. "I'd rather go to my place," she said.

"Oh, do you have your own place?" Conner asked. "I mean, we don't want to piss someone off if we're going to do this stuff." He was into doing whatever she wanted but he was feeling strange about driving. It seemed like he was going so much faster than everyone else and his little Rabbit was feeling like a Cadillac. He was suddenly low to the ground in the thing. His ass was almost touching the asphalt and his feet hovered over his body instead of on the pedals. They were being pulled by a cable connected to the power lines. *Yeah.* He was a fucking bus driver!

"I need more and I just want you to come to my place anyway," she said. "I'm only about ten blocks from here."

Conner drove the ten blocks, which turned into sixteen blocks and felt like fifty, his car like one of those long drag racing vehicles, except wobbling through space. The parachute billowing behind them, shadowing their bodies. He was almost embarrassed about the parachute.

"I'm not Krystal," the girl said. "I'm just the bait."

What? Conner felt something disconnect in him, his brain lost. "What is Krystal? Who is Krystal?" he said, and laughed uneasily. Some of the drug was out on a plate on a low wooden coffee table in front of him. He sat directly in the middle of the leather couch, staring at it and trying to estimate how long he was going to be messed up.

"Krystal's my mom," she said.

Conner groaned and rested his head on his shoulder. The girl came over and caressed his cheeks. She leaned against him and he opened one eye to see down her thin red shirt. It was like a doily and it glowed burgundy on her chest, her orange nipples.

More powder in his nose.

His weekend was over. Where had it gone? He hadn't even found time to call his daughter or his daughter's angry mother. Instead, he seemed to be watching things happen to him in slow motion. Things he couldn't stop or for some reason he didn't care to stop. He was in a clean room now, a woman's room. In a bed. There was an older woman next to him. They were both wet with sweat and other moisture. The woman was most likely in her 50s, old enough to have veins everywhere he looked. To have teeth that didn't seem real. Teeth that seemed to dangle over him as she rode him in an unsteady manic rhythm. The woman did everything she could do to him, pushed him into every part of her. She pressed his chubby belly with her own swollen breasts. She worked him like a chore. Until she was done.

Conner stumbled out of the apartment as another morning started somewhere on the calendar. Did he have to be at work tonight? Or did he have one more day? He had to find a newspaper or something. A friendly stranger? *"Excuse me, can you tell me what day it is?"* What did he think he was, a hostage?

He enjoyed himself anyway, or at least he thought he probably did. He thought about the man with the hearing aid shot out, shouting for help and God damn. The white suit splattered with paint. It was a disgrace. An embarrassment. A pathetic attempt at sport that turned into pleading. A bad game that turned worse.

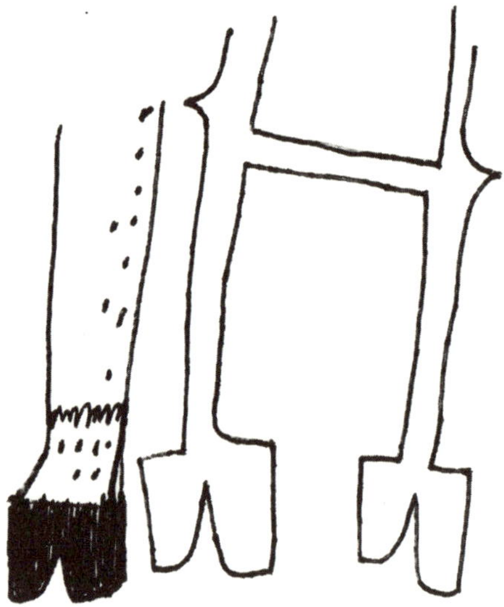

hoof letter

EVERYTHING

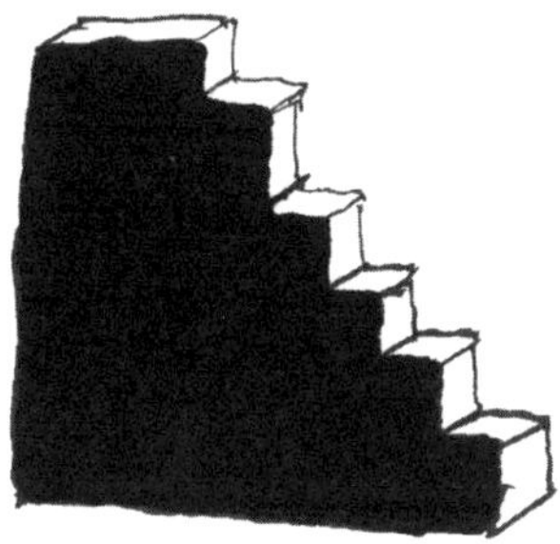

IS HUNGRY

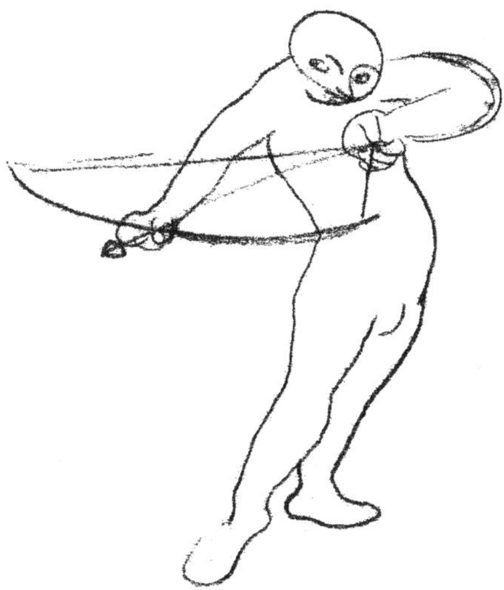

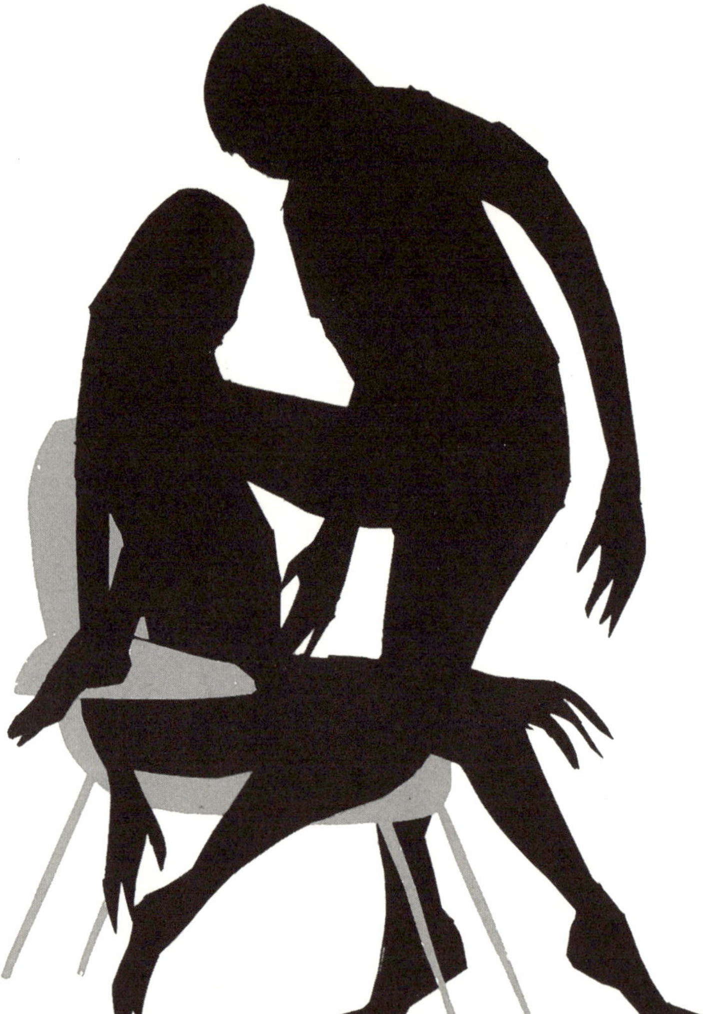

I never asked to be Solid Boy, the Boy of Unusual Mass. Given a list of lifelong gifts to choose from, I don't think too many folks would pick "density." But what's the old saying? Some heroes are born, some heroes are made through circumstance, and some heroes are created in freak lab accidents?

Me, I was just born. No shattered test tubes, no commingled chemicals, no lightning strike at the moment of impossible odds. No ka-boom. Just a routine check-up. I was twelve. The doctor stopped me as I pulled my shirt back on.

You are a boy of unusual mass, he said—Well, all right. If that's the diagnosis, that's the diagnosis. I don't think "diagnosis" is Latin for "guess" or "options." My parents said they'd support me whatever my decision, but I knew they were secretly proud. Once the word came down, did I have any other choice than the academy, the team assignment, the costume fitting?

Some people say that once they've been in this for awhile, they can't imagine any other life. But that hasn't happened to me yet.

CUTLASS AND SOLID BOY

by Adam Sternbergh

The trouble with being Solid Boy is that you're always being thrown through things. That's your power. Especially when you're assigned to a team with a guy called The Catapult. That's no coincidence, believe me.

We're supposed to work together, but I don't like him much. Not because he chucks me through walls and such, but because he insists on being costumed like a cat, with a tail and whiskers and everything.

"It's right there in my name," he says.

"But it's nothing to do with cats," I say, lying cradled in the crook of his overlong hurling arm, my knees pulled up to my chest. "You're like a catapult. You see? The two things are not related."

"Yeah, well, call me when you can do something besides being solid," he says, then flings me through the brick wall of an abandoned factory. Inside, bad guys scramble, leaving steaming coffee mugs and their plans spread out on the table. My team charges in through the me-shaped hole while I stand and dust myself off.

Cutlass is my girlfriend. They discourage inter-team dating, but even so. You spend so much time together, it's hard to avoid.

She also has naming issues. Ask her and she'll tell you it's Cut Lass, two separate words. I told her that doesn't make sense and she hacked at me with her sword, albeit playfully.

I was attracted to her at first because of that billowing shirt. I'll admit it. It's a pirate-style thing with ruffles and it's cut really low in the front. She asked them to lower it when she had it tailored. She's not shy about that sort of thing. They give you a certain amount of costuming input at the initial fittings. And they're always happy to up the sexy-quotient, which plays well to the crowds.

When she really gets going, scissor-kicking and pounding on crooks and slicing at the air with that sabre, all those ruffles and that lace at her neck start to move like white smoke, and she looks like a genie loosed from a lamp, come to grant wishes.

I told her that once and she said, "Sure, if your wish is for an ass-kicking," and laughed.

She doesn't have natural powers. She's classified as "Orphan/Avenger." She trained herself to fight after watching her parents die. Most orphan/avenger cases involve parental death as a result of crime, a mugging gone wrong or what have you. But her folks passed on within months of each other due to unrelated illnesses. No ka-boom for her either. Just a bad coincidence.

She was six, and she took to the gym. Her family wasn't all that well off from what I understand. No private facilities in the mansion basement. Instead, she haunted the Y. It's not really clear how she fed herself or educated herself in between all those late-night gymnastics training sessions and swordplay tutorials and sharpshooting drills, or who exactly took care of her. Apparently, she found a blind mentor. He was an old guy with stubble who hung around the heavy bag and had empty bottles on his breath. He taught her a few things. But she doesn't much like to talk about those years and I don't press.

But don't think you can tease her about her lack of powers. Orphan/avengers usually take a lot of flack from the natural-borns. Take our strong guy, whose name is Oak and who's made out of wood. Don't worry—he can walk and talk and smile and all that, and he's got a sprout of leaves covering his groin area, like the Jolly Green Giant. And he's smooth like a polished wooden bannister, not rough like bark. He's really strong, though, like a tree would be, I guess, if it was shaped like a person. Fire is his weakness. Well, duh.

Oak used to bust Cutlass' chops about not being natural-born. Early on, when we were first assembled, he used to go at her about it day after day. Plus, he'd always make these bad jokes about "sporting wood." I think he had a thing for her then. So when he took his two-week vacation, she filled his locker with tent caterpillars. When he got back he swung the locker door open and found it infested with creepy-crawlies and their cobwebbed tents, strung like ghostly cotton candy. We all howled, but he was petrified. He pissed sap down his leg, I shit you not.

Plus, Cutlass has her days. She gets in black moods and then we all sit around and silently pray for a siren. Dam break, jail break—any kind of break. Otherwise, we're just stuck inside playing cards and no one saying anything.

Get to know me and eventually you'll ask: Did I ever think of going the other way? Not that I have a particular bad streak. I think you'd eventually ask that of anyone. We're contractually forbidden from discussing it publicly, but we talk about it among ourselves. The Aerie told me once that he'd considered it. We were up in the sleeping quarters and he was grooming his falcon, and I was on my cot. Sparrows circled The Aerie's head, like usual. A couple of cockatiels screeched and poked around for crumbs over in the kitchenette, shitting on everything. He said at times he'd wished that he and his bird servants lived alone in the mountains, plotting evil capers.

"I even sketched out plans for a secret hideaway," he said, pulling some sheets of paper from the foot locker at the end of his cot. I was having trouble hearing him over the cawing of the various birds. He was supposedly controlling them all mentally but it's not like he keeps them on a tight leash. Witness the shit-drips everywhere.

"I'm no architect," he said, unfolding one sheet with a schematic sketched on it. "They're just harmless doodles, fantasies. I'd christened it with a name, though: Sanctuary." Sure enough, it said "Sanctuary" across the top of the sheet in meticulous calligraphy.

The Aerie's full name is Lord Albert Alfred something. I hear he grew up in a castle. As we spoke about his hideaway, he was wearing his full eagle-head mask, so it was impossible to see from his face if he was kidding or not.

"So what do you do?" is the other thing people ask me, mostly at the conventions and the card-signing shows.

"I'm a boy of unusual mass," I say. Kids usually look at me blankly, then shrug and plunk down their pile of thirty or forty Solid Boy trading cards for me to sign. A Solid Boy card is worth about 40 cents, a little more for the rookie card. But signed, they fetch a buck.

"There's a ten-card signing limit," I say.

"Whatever. I'm just killing time until the lineup for Master Man clears," they say.

What I do is get thrown through walls, and deflect bullets, and get swung by Oak over his head like a human mace whenever a crowd of henchmen converge on us. I can punch people, but it's not like I'm particularly strong. My muscles are just tough, like a really hard rubber ball, and I don't feel pain. I tried to bulk up but the doctors told me don't bother. Because my muscles are of such unusual mass, they can't be built up through normal weight-training. So I keep myself in trim shape through bike riding and squash, and leave the strong man stuff to Oak.

He's pretty good at wielding me. There's a real trick to grabbing someone's ankles and swinging them around in circles over your head. The first time we tried it I puked, and like a jackass he kept windmilling me so that barf sprayed everywhere like a lawn sprinkler. We've smoothed out the rough edges since then. The effect is not as spectacular, of course, as that achieved by the actual The Human Mace when he's swung over the head of Iron Age, the strong guy for Team Power Five. And, admittedly, Oak pretty much stole their move after he saw them doing it on TV on the nightly-news round-up. We got a cease-and-desist order from Team Power Five, so now we have to be discreet about it.

I block bullets because, unlike most other team's strong guys, Oak can't get shot. Which is to say, he can, but he doesn't much like it. Iron Age, for example, has skin of iron, so bullets bounce off. On Oak, bullets leave pockmarks. Plus, when he gets shot, he bleeds sap, like a tapped tree.

One time, we were busting up a bank robbery and we burst in to a barrage of bullets. Cutlass kicked ass and The Aerie unleashed the birds. We punched and pecked the hell out of them, then hogtied them in a bunch in the middle of the bank floor. Once we'd rounded up the hoodlums, though, we found Oak curled in a corner by the manager's office. He was ass-down in a puddle of sap, bawling. Bullet holes cratered his chest like bad acne.

We plugged him up with epoxy resin. Regardless, I don't mind taking bullet-blocking duty because I'm usually looking for something to do in any case.

We needed another woman. Our membership was unbalanced as it was, with five guys and one woman, and then The Lemur bolted. Our outfit, Team Justice Busters, doesn't have much clout since we operate mainly as a farm team for other, more established teams. No one calls us a farm team officially, but that's the reality. What else would you call it when The Lemur gets a call one day and by the following week we spot him lunching with Master Man and now he's a full-fledged fighter in Team Gang Nitro? And we're down from six members to five at the height of blackout season?

So we needed a new member anyway and it would be nice if she was a lady. We had a strong guy, an animal manipulator, a hand-to-hand fighter, a non-lethal projectiles guy, and me, wherever I fit in. The projectile, I guess. We didn't have a leader, though, since The Lemur left, and he wasn't much for making decisions anyway. I hoped for another woman, but Cutlass wasn't excited.

"What do we need? Who exactly are they going to send us?" she said, layering her toast with slabs of cold butter. Normally she eats her toast dry. The jodhpurs they costumed her in are tight and unforgiving. Why jodhpurs for a pirate, I'm not sure.

But she keeps sticks of butter in the fridge for a treat. When she starts laying down butter-pats in thick bricks like paving stones, punishing the toast, that means she's thinking, Fuck it, fuck the jodhpurs, nothing matters anymore.

She laid down butter blocks. "The five of us are fine."

"We could use another woman," I said. "Plus, blackout season."

"Yes, that's exactly what we fucking need," she said, and took a big bite of the toast. "They could send us a fucking super dog with healing breath and X-ray farts and you'd fucking clap your hands with glee, wouldn't you?"

"You know, we're just talking and all the swearing doesn't help," I said.

"Yes, but I'm a fucking pirate, remember?" She put the half-eaten toast on the counter and left. For a second I had the urge to save the slice in a Ziploc. Her teeth had made a perfect imprint of her biteplate in the butter, suitable for forensic identification should anything ever happen to her.

The Central Office faxed over details of our new assignee. Her name was Psiren, with a silent P, and her mind controlled men. This was good news: a mentallist *and* a woman.

"What's her name?" Cutlass said. "Psiren?" She kept pronouncing it to sound like "piss iron."

The Aerie's birds squalled and fluttered around the training room, trailing puffs of downy feathers like dirty snow. The other, more high-profile teams got high-tech facilities with computerized training programs and holographic monsters. We had a second-floor gym with poor ventilation and a rowing machine. Our HQ was housed in an old fire station, freed up by municipal layoffs. Every new member made a big deal of complaining, slamming their locker door for the first few weeks and muttering about "whatever I did to draw *this* chickenshit crew." Eventually, though, they'd settle in. Me, I secretly liked it. The firehall was a beautiful brick building with high ceilings, and we got a fire pole. Besides, I never grew up dreaming of joining a team so I had no expectations.

You stay out of my locker, I stay out of your locker, everybody happy.

"What's her profile?" asked The Catapult.

"She dresses like a cat," said Cutlass. "Now we have two of you."

"I'm the cat in this group," said The Catapult and stroked his pipe-cleaner whiskers. Of course, he hadn't been issued a cat costume. The cat modifications were all homemade. Central Office discourages modifications officially, but in most cases they'll turn a blind eye.

There wasn't much for The Catapult to do during training sessions. He usually sat in the corner and chatted with us, his overlong hurling arm curled at his side. The curse of the overlong hurling arm is that he can only use it for hurling. Otherwise it just lies there, limp and flat like an unrolled firehose.

"Yeah, Piss Iron is french for Alley Cat," said Cutlass, between shadow-boxing jabs. "You know that, right? She's like an alley cat. She makes this terrible screeching noise and then sprays her enemies with piss."

"Why are they sending us another cat?" he said, wounded.

"Maybe they want us to have one cat-person who's not a secret fag," said Oak. He didn't train much either. Mostly we all just sat around and watched Cutlass work the heavy bag.

This is the point at which our leader, if we had one, would step in and say, "All right, you two, cut it out." But as I outlined earlier, our team is currently leaderless. So

The Aerie just pretended to be distracted by his bird, chucking the falcon's chin, and I said nothing as well. The Aerie's sparrows twittered.

Cutlass let loose a series of roundhouse kicks at the heavy bag, grunting like a tennis player. Then she held out her hand and I passed her a towel and she said, "Can we cut it out with these fucking birds?"

There's only one woman who Cutlass ever got along with, that I know of. Her name was Airheart and she was a flyer. Flyers are the rarest type. Airheart wore a white silk scarf, like an old-fashioned pilot, and a leather cap and goggles. The airmen's get-up was just a costuming flourish; she had no plane, of course. She'd just straighten out her body and go.

Normally, they would have fast-tracked someone like that straight through to a top-level team, flyers being so in-demand. But Airheart was a widow. She lost her husband just a few months before her assignment. He flipped his snowmobile into a crevice near a mountain pass. She flew for three days trying to find him, searching the snow for trails. Eventually they had to use dog teams to sniff him out.

Our crew was meant to serve as a low-stress halfway house to ease her into her assignment, or so the reasoning went.

Under her cap, she wore a page-boy haircut that got all staticky and stuck to her cheeks. She was thin and looked glamourous like a flapper, though she never got excited or danced. She never even raised her voice, which with our team is a real feat. She seemed like a retired flapper, now out of the life and unflappable. When Oak went too far grilling her once about what brand of snowmobile it was, because certain makes will tip right over if you don't know what you're doing, she just smiled sadly and said she'd really rather not discuss it, then asked the Catapult if he had any hobbies.

She and Cutlass hit it off straight away. They spent hours talking out on the patio and they made for a funny pair: Airheart in her leather pilot's cap, Cutlass with her coal-coloured curls and ruffled shirt. We figured they got along so well because Cutlass was starved for a girl's company. She'd been stuck with us boys for so long. But when I asked Cutlass once what they talked about so much, she said, "Mostly phantom limbs." At first, I thought she meant some supervillain I hadn't heard of yet.

Then one day Cutlass woke up and Airheart had disappeared. The official report was stamped LOAM: Lost On A Mission, but if Airheart took off on a mission, she didn't tell any of us. She never reported for her next posting. I broached it with Cutlass once and even though I tried to bring it up gingerly she said, "Why in the fuck do you think she would have told fucking me?" then vanished into the gym for the rest of the afternoon. You could hear the thumps on the heavy bag all through the house, like cries from a torture chamber.

Psiren wore a gold costume with scales on it like a

mermaid, and no mask. She had blonde hair and she was perfectly toned. Her costume fit like a leotard and was slit in a V down the front, and had a little upturned collar, and ended at her feet in dainty high-heeled boots, also gold.

"I'll take a slice of that," Oak murmured to me when she showed up and dropped her duffel bag and took her first look around. The Aerie tried to act like a lord, taking her bag and bowing and kissing her hand and she smiled at him but wasn't interested. Plus, with him you can always tell his true emotional state because of how the birds are acting. As he tried to calmly escort her to the sleeping quarters, the birds were shrieking and flying in circles and humping each other in the rafters.

"So, can you tell what I'm thinking right now?" Oak said at dinner. We ate at a long cafeteria-style table, mostly microwave pizza. But in honour of the new member we'd ordered in Chinese. You got a daily meal stipend if you want to go out and eat somewhere fancy, but you can't sit in a restaurant without being pestered by fans. So we made do with pizza or, on special occasions, Chinese.

"I'm pretty new to all this, but I think I have an idea," Psiren said. She'd pushed her pizza aside after one polite bite. She turned and looked past me toward Cutlass. I'd sat between them, on purpose. "And what's your name again?" she asked.

"Cutlass."

"Cutlass, like the car?" Psiren said. "Like Cutlass Sierra? That's an excellent name, Cutlass Sierra. That would be a really cool porn-star name."

"It's a fucking pirate name," said Cutlass, and I got ready to stick my solid arms in the air in case she lost it. I knew I should have enforced the No Swords At The Table rule.

"And you're obviously a master of birds," she said to The Aerie. He blushed. He wasn't wearing his eagle-head mask, out of politeness, I guess. But it meant you could see his ruddy drunkard's face, which was now even more red and inflamed.

"Yeah, he's always trying to take control of my wood pecker," Oak said and rapped sharply on the underside of the table.

Psiren smiled. "And you're some sort of cat?" she said to The Catapult.

"That's right," he said. He pawed a pipe-cleaner. "I'm The Catapult."

"I'm going to call you Felix," she purred.

Cutlass and I never had any privacy, since we all slept in cots in the common sleeping room. On my first few nights with the team, all the snoring and snuffling and bird-chirps kept me awake. By now I was inured to it. Cutlass never slept much anyway, her whole life.

We whispered, crammed together into one cot like stowaways.

"Now that there's six of us, maybe you and I can

take a weekend off together," I said. We'd often talked about saving up and pooling our stipends to get a hotel room for a weekend, but with only five members we could never synch up our vacation time. "We should do it now, before, you know, there's any change in the situation."

There'd been rumours for awhile that Cutlass might be recruited for another, more high-profile outfit. Team The Awesome Thunder had been sniffing around. There weren't many woman orphan/avengers available, and they'd lost the She-Beast when she blew out a knee playing Ultimate frisbee.

"Yes, or we could quit," she said. She often talked about quitting.

"Okay, but then what do we do? Work? I don't have any life skills." I'd skipped high school to join the training academy. My schooling was something of a disappointment. They'd promised top-notch academics, but the teachers looked the other way. The classrooms were chaos: kids fighting, flying, setting fires with heat vision.

"Did I say anything about fucking working?" She was getting angry. I knew where this was headed. She'd get too mad to talk, then go smoke out the window. I'd lie still for a few token minutes, then slide back over into my own cot.

"If you want to leave, we can leave," I said. "I'll leave. But we should wait until after blackout season."

"Didn't we have this conversation last year?" she said.

I tried to make her smile. "We're a couple of freaks. Why don't we run away and join the circus?"

"We're already in the fucking circus."

We both lay silent for a moment. Pigeons cooed in the rafters. There was a spat-spat-spatting sound, somewhere close to us.

"I can't fucking believe this," she said, and swung out of the bed. She leaned over me and whispered, "I trained since I was six fucking years old. Six." She straightened up to leave, then bent over me again. "If I'd spent that time learning a fucking instrument, don't you think I'd be the best fucking violinist in the world right now?"

Then she said loudly, "Birds are shitting on us so why am I fucking whispering!" Then she left and slammed the door. In another cot, Oak snorted. I lay for a moment longer, then patted my face and arms and torso and legs to see if I'd been hit by the falling guano.

Given the tension in the group, I was happy to welcome the first blackout weekend. It was hot as a kiln and we all needed to vent.

They organize blackout season every year. It's mostly a show for the fans. Central Office waits for the hottest weekend of the summer, then shuts down whole blocks on the city grid. Then they open the prisons and loose the bad guys. We swoop in and mop up. Sure, a few windows get smashed and some stereos get snatched, but on the whole it's good for the morale of the average Joe.

From time to time, a talk-radio host complains

about the whole charade and exhorts the public to action, but for the most part the people enjoy it. They mill about in the streets, drinking beers, and then cheer when a fight breaks out. They love when we pound on felons. As for the big-mouthed talk-show host, after a reasonable amount of time has passed, he's quietly replaced by someone who focuses more on local sports.

Our biggest problem is stumbling around in the dark. Teams smack into other teams. We're all supposed to stick to our designated quadrants, but some teams are glory hogs. I've even seen a few team members hoarding their own stolen loot. I once tried to stop The Hydrant when I caught him slipping out of a vault with safety-deposit boxes under each arm. I just wanted a word with him. But he turned and loosed a torrent from his mid-section that doused me and sent me flying. I don't know what it was, but it didn't smell like water.

The siren went off, interrupting our game of Risk. We checked the city map. A red light flashed on an intersection about two blocks from our HQ. The Museum of Natural History.

"Fucking museum jobs," said Oak. "This whole thing is so transparent."

Another disadvantage for Team Justice Busters was that we didn't have a flyer. After Airheart vanished, we put in for a minivan, but then Oak burned the clutch out practicing a bootlegger's reverse in the parking lot. The

Aerie used to ride his ostriches to crime scenes until he put on so much weight.

We headed down to the street corner and waved for a cab.

The Catapult unfurled his noodle arm. Besides hurling things, this was about all he was good for. Still, a couple of taxis zipped by without slowing, their drivers looking wary. Team members are notorious for stiffing.

The Catapult turned and started to say, "I think we should just walk it," when suddenly a checker cab stopped with a jolt at the curb.

"Thank you," said Psiren into the driver's side window. The driver smiled a wobbly grin, as though drunk.

"Will he take all six of us?" asked The Aerie.

We sewed up the museum job fairly easily. To be honest, museum mop-ups are considered a bit embarrassing. After all, when you throw open the doors to a prison, what kind of crooks head straight for the priceless pottery shards? Not the cold killers, that's for sure.

I caught up with Psiren in the Roman Empire section. A gang of six crooks were standing around her, while she told a story. They were shuffling their feet and she was touching her hair. She gave me a look as I passed, and I almost stayed to listen in. But I thought I should check and make sure everyone had enough plastic handcuffs.

The only snag we hit was when Oak had to pry Cutlass off a guy who she'd pinned to the floor in the Glory of the Ottomans section, and was just waling on.

"He fucking broke a vase!" she said, almost shrieking, as Oak hefted her in the air. "These are fucking antiquities!" The guy just lay there, gurgling.

"Ease off," Oak said.

"Fuck him. Break him, he'll fucking mend," she said.

"So that was fun," Psiren said, leaning on the railing of the deck. We had a small patio off the dining room. Oak built it during one slow summer and The Aerie sprung for a couple of plastic chairs.

"Were you nervous?" I asked.

"No," she said. "It all comes pretty easy to me."

"I guess the academy does a good job of prepping us," I said. "You know, for the various situations."

"I wouldn't know. I never went. I just got into this a year ago."

"What happened?" I lowered my voice to sound comforting. "Freak accident?"

"No, nothing like that," she said. "This is how it's been my whole life. I guess I just never thought of it as, you know, whatever. A power." When she said "power," she shook her hands in front of her like Al Jolson. Then she touched her hair.

"Let me show you something," she said. She ducked through the screen door and I followed. She sat on the edge of her cot and unzipped her duffel.

"Check this out," she said. She unfolded a series of graph-paper sheets, connected so you can feed them through a printer. Colourful lines crisscrossed the length of the sheet, then crested right off the page.

"My brain scan," she said. "They ran a bunch of tests on me. They stuck those electrode things all over my head and chest, and then had me tell a few stories to a pair of security guards. That's this part—" she pointed to where the lines sailed off the page. "When they checked the readout, the doctor okayed me on the spot. He signed a sheet so I could skip the training school, too. After the preliminary physicals and fittings, they sent me straight here. He was so nice about it," she said.

"That's cool." I thought back to my six years at the academy, dodging flaming spit balls and getting pantsed by kids who took off at superspeed.

"Just think." She folded the paper back up and closed up the duffel bag. "A year ago I was bartending. Can you believe that? But I had a feeling something like this would happen, you know?"

"Not really," I said. She laughed.

"What's your power?" she said.

If you're going to get caught cheating on your girlfriend, don't get caught this way: Where your girlfriend walks in and flicks on the lights to find you drunk on margaritas and humping the new team member on a cot in the communal sleeping area. Actually, she never turned on the lights. She just kept flicking the switch. It was a blackout, and our grid was the one that got shut down.

This wasn't the worst thing anyone's ever walked in on in our communal sleeping area. There was the time a few of us got back early from a sold-out movie to find

The Aerie naked in his cot with his eagle mask on and a bunch of doves nesting in his crotch. And Oak is always getting caught with some groupie's head buried in his leafy patch. But this time was up there among the worst, for sure.

I stopped in mid-hump and held my breath in the dark, as though caught in the middle of a push-up. Cutlass toggled the light switch. It stayed dark. We'd all hunkered down for the night because of the blackout and a serious storm. It was the end of the season so the other teams could handle what few alarms there'd be. Oak and The Aerie were playing Sorry in the dining room and Cutlass was supposedly working out and The Catapult was off somewhere and Psiren had blended a batch of margaritas that we'd been enjoying on the patio, watching the heavy rain.

The light switch made a clicking sound. It click-clicked like a cigarette lighter trying to sprout a flame. No lights, but she kept flicking.

We didn't breathe. My arms started to wobble, holding all my weight.

Then: ka-boom. A lightning flash, as bright as flood-lights through the firehouse windows. The thunder crash came a second later, long after Psiren and I had been caught in our sweaty tableau, flash-frozen on the cot as though snared, naked and guilty, in the burst of a private eye's flashbulb.

We had a guy in our group once named The Cuckold. He

was only around for a few weeks. He wore a jester's hat with little jingling bells on it. We never figured out what his powers were. He just sat in the corner, crying quietly. Then he up and moved west, Seattle I think.

I don't know why she should be so mad. I mean, of course I know why, but even so. She humped every guy in the group within two months of joining before she got to me, Oak included. She even humped The Catapult the night of our team Christmas party. Plus, she humped guys from other teams too. She humped Mister Mach and The Tendril and I'm pretty sure she humped Justice, and that's just the ones I know about. I'm just who she got attached to.

I only complained about her history once, a long time before the lightning and the push-ups and the cot.

"But you're the guy I stuck with," she said.

"Or got stuck with," I said.

When we used to have sex, we'd start by laughing and making stupid jokes. "Come on, Cut Lass," I'd say. "Cut loose, Cutlass." Then she'd grab my boner and say, "Yep, that's solid boy."

She'd only ever sit on top, pinning me like a wrestler. You might think it was a power thing, but that wasn't the case. She let the other guys hump her the other way, them on top, looming over her, but she said she hated it because it felt like a coffin lid closing. With me, she said, she had something solid to hold on to. She'd squat on me and hook her fingers into my rubber-ball shoulders.

"This way, you're like my flutterboard," she said. "I'm the castaway and you're the piece of debris."

When I humped Psiren, we did it the coffin-lid way.

To tell the truth, I felt like a pro, leaning all my weight on my arms while the cot wobbled and Psiren moaned. But I don't know if that feeling was me, or something she was making me feel with her mind.

We tried to talk it out one last time. We went out to the patio and locked the screen door.

"You have to understand," I said. "She has this power."

I tried bringing up all the guys from Cutlass's past, but she made wet, choking sounds. Then she just let me have it, blow after blow, right in the kisser.

It didn't hurt. I couldn't even feel it. That's the upside of being Solid Boy. Still, I thought: This can't be healthy.

"Cutlass," I said. "Stop punching my face."

She took off, her locker emptied out. Somehow she even managed to take the heavy bag. Just the chain remained, dangling freely from the ceiling.

We thought she might resurface with another team, but never heard anything. Psiren guessed she'd turned lesbo and split with her secret honey. Then Psiren informed us she'd signed on with Team The Awesome Thunder and this was her two-weeks notice. So we were left the four of us, unbalanced and understaffed, with no leader and no women.

Oak made noises at the dinner table about tracking down Cutlass. Central Office offered extra-generous bounties for team members gone the other way. They were happy to have us street-fight with ex-cons and thugs, but they knew that if too many team members switched over, there'd be real chaos to contend with.

"Let her show her face at just one heist," Oak said. "I'll crack her like she needs to be cracked."

I never worried that he'd actually do it. She knew his weakness, after all. She knew all of our weaknesses. With Oak it was fire, and that was just the beginning. The Catapult cowered at loud noises. Psiren could only control men, of course, and last I heard, she'd got cut up badly by a female turncoat named Catfight. With The Aerie, you just had to catch one of his birds and wrap your hands around its fragile little neck, and he'd call off the whole flock. As for me, I don't have a weakness that I know of. Then again, I can't do much to begin with.

We always wondered, as we watched her pummel the heavy bag or sail into a mob of crooks with her sabre blade flashing, what her weakness might be. That's the one piece of info they don't fax over with your profile. Instead, the weaknesses are all encrypted on a hard-drive at Central Office, so that only they know them. Just in case one day they need to rein you in.

But she could tell yours just from meeting you once. She had a knack for it and now I think that maybe that was hers. She saw weaknesses, all the time. She'd shake your hand and know. Turns out she was natural-born after all, for all of Oak's taunting.

When Oak talked of catching her, we'd all nod along but say nothing. We didn't want to encourage him, but didn't mind listening to him prattle on while we waited for the pizza to cool. It's not that we thought we couldn't find her. We just knew there wasn't one of us who could take her on if we did.

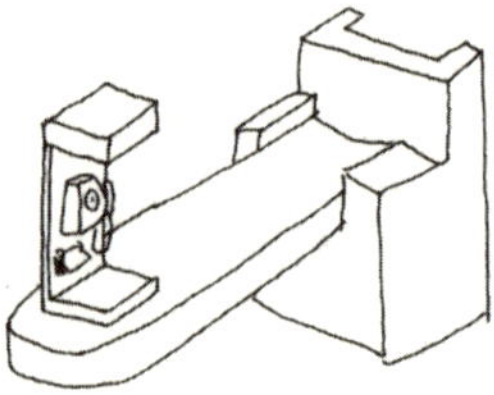

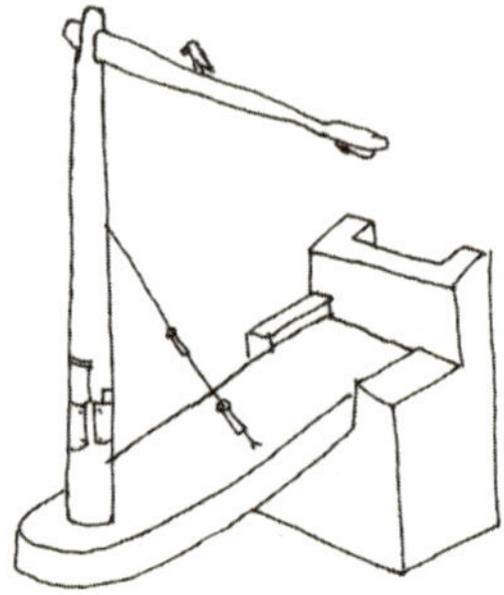

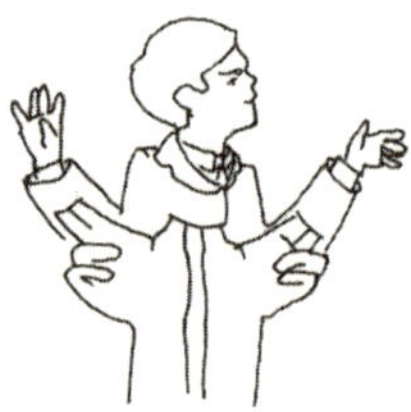

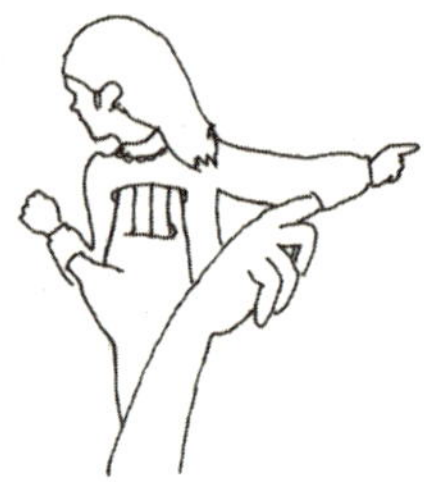

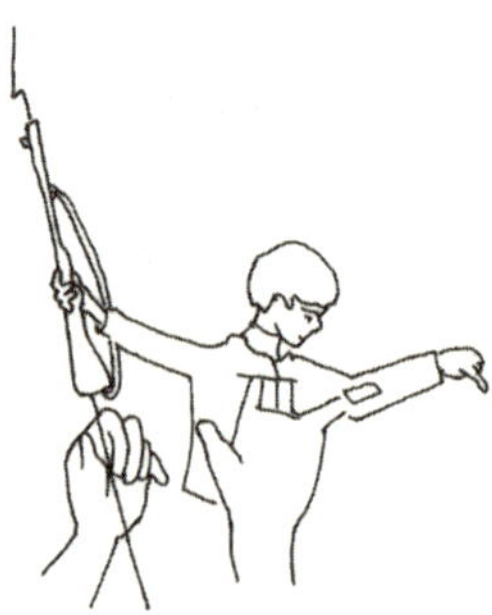

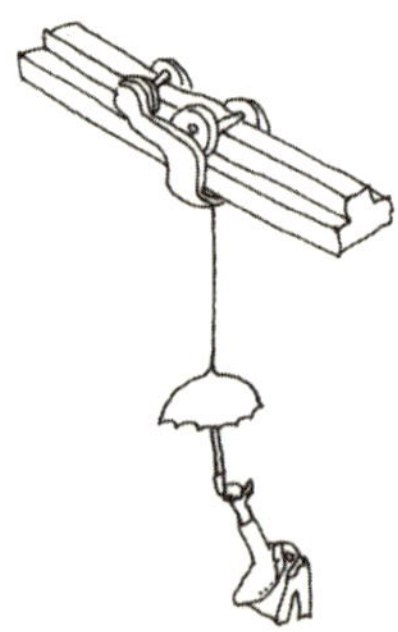

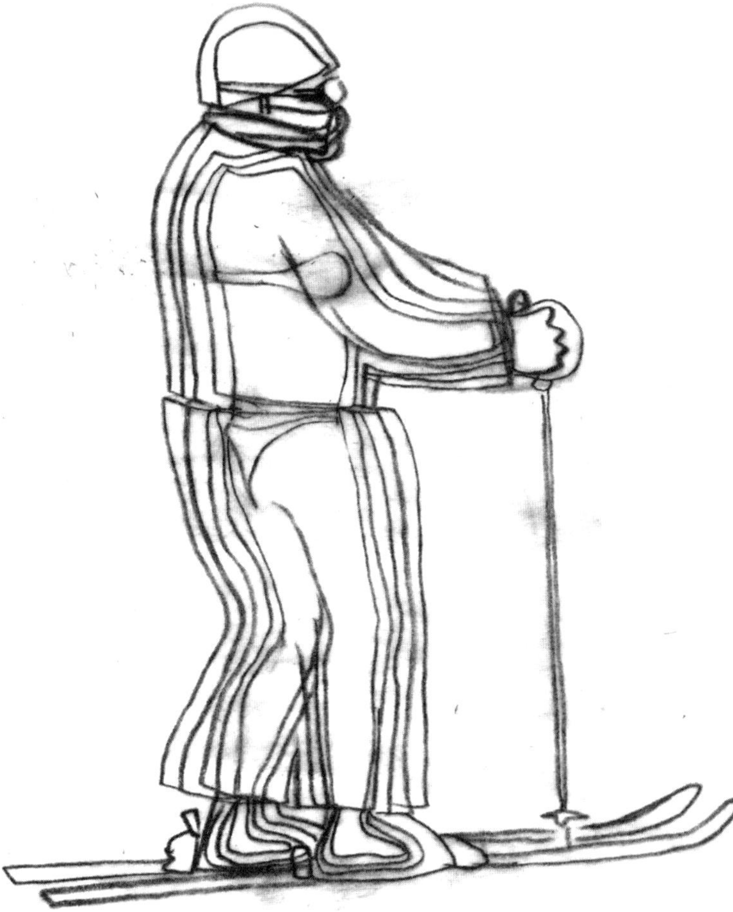

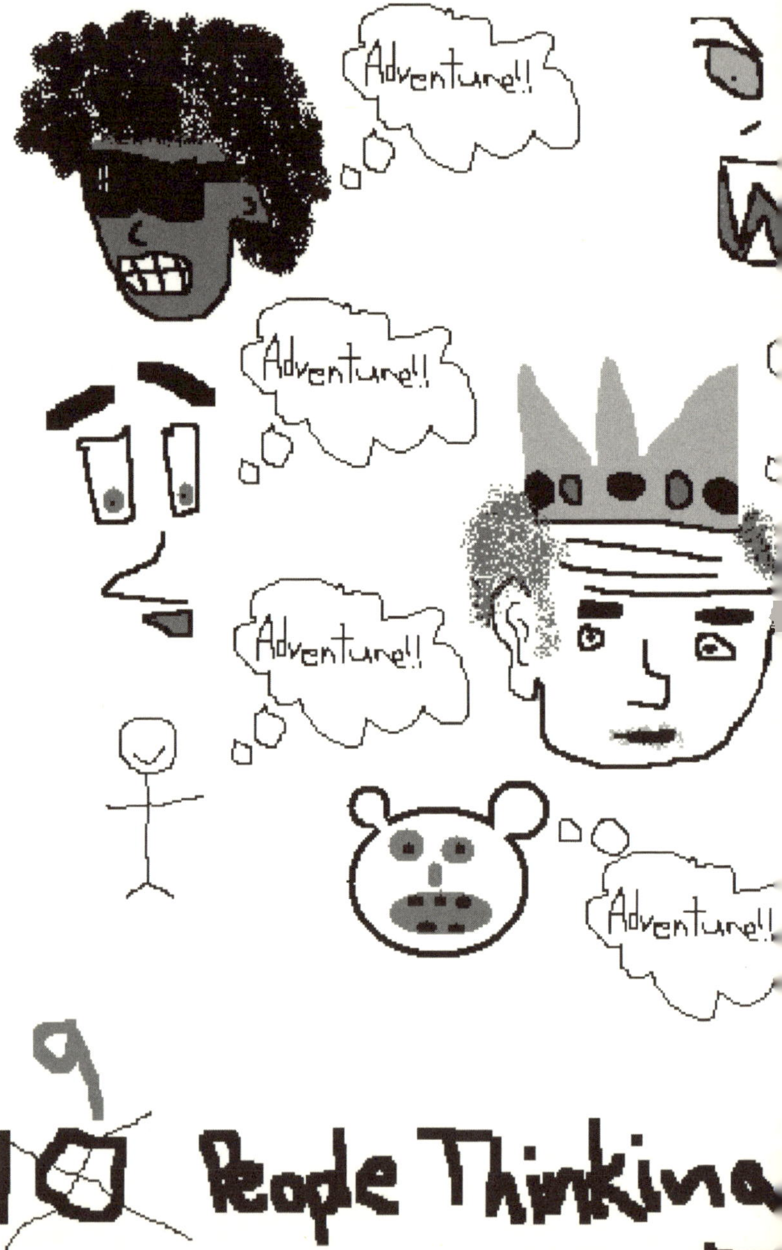
Adventure!!
Adventure!!
Adventure!!
Adventure!!
9
People Thinking

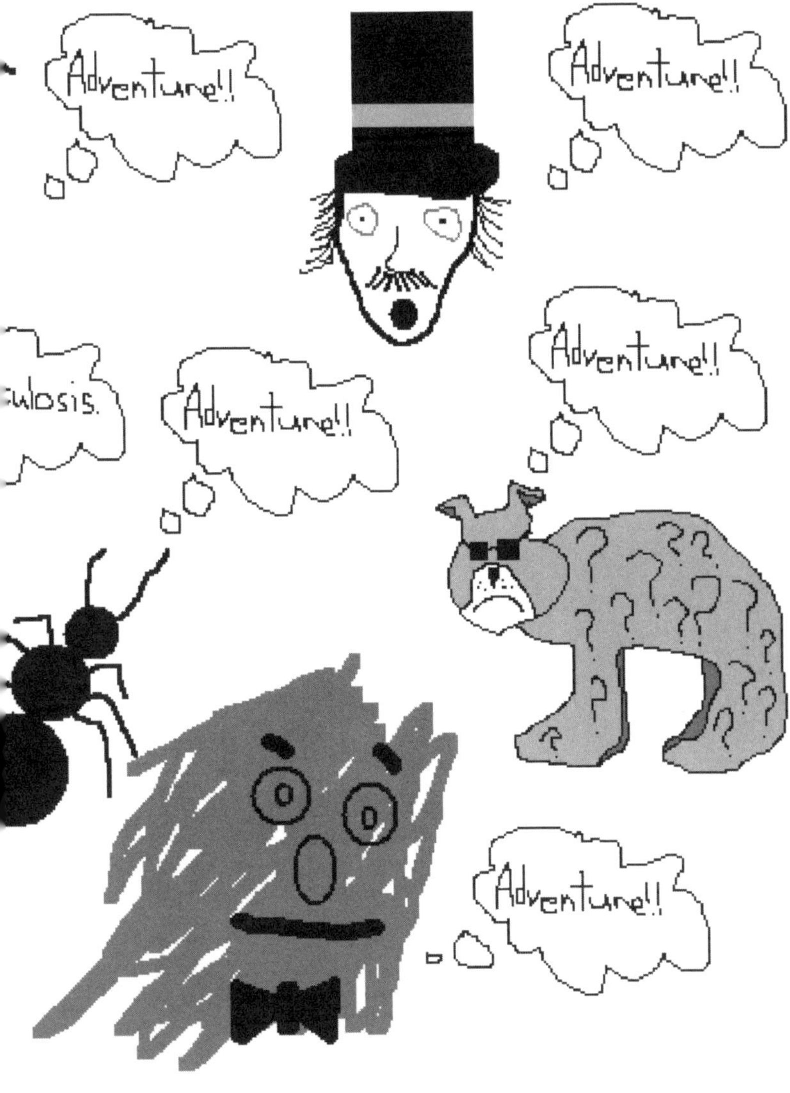

bout Adventure.

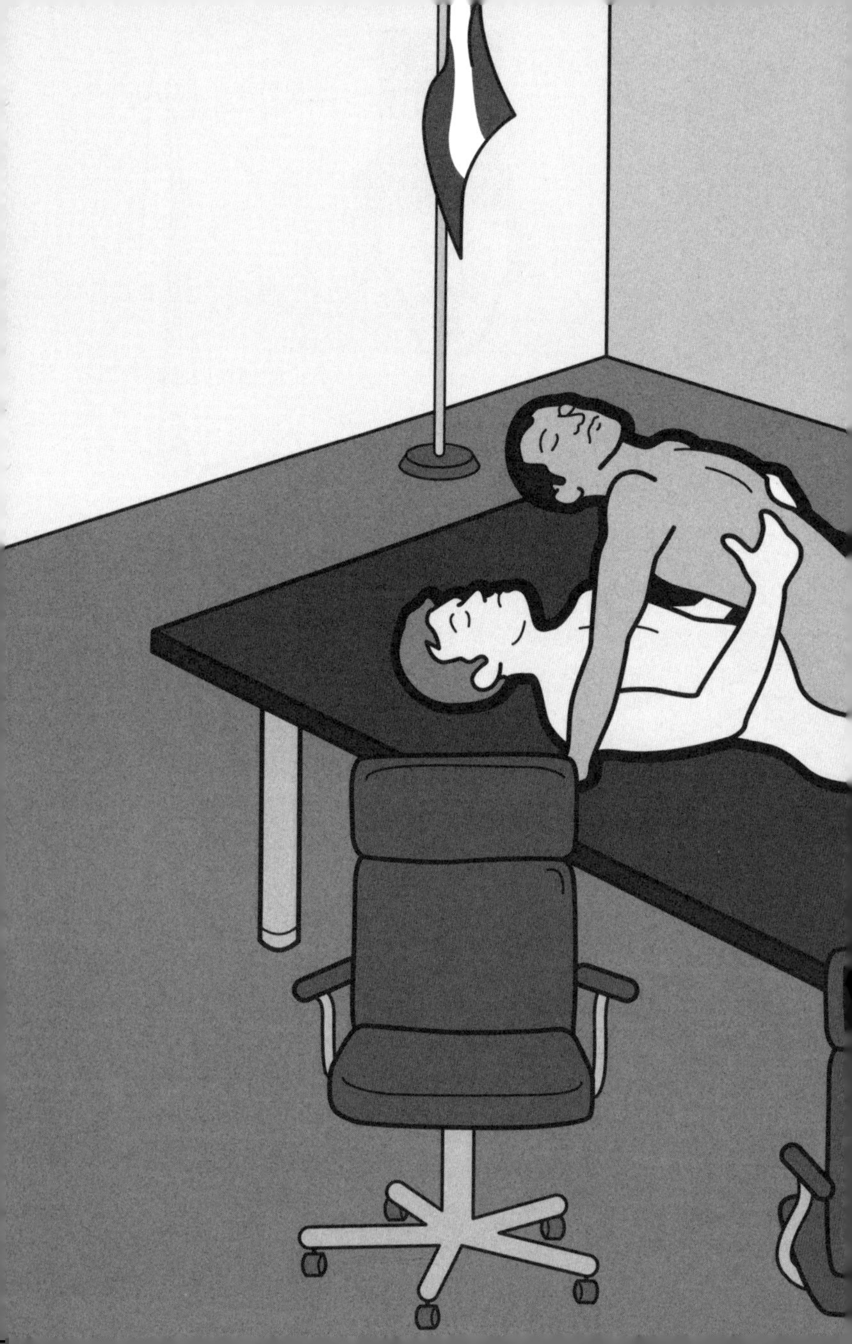

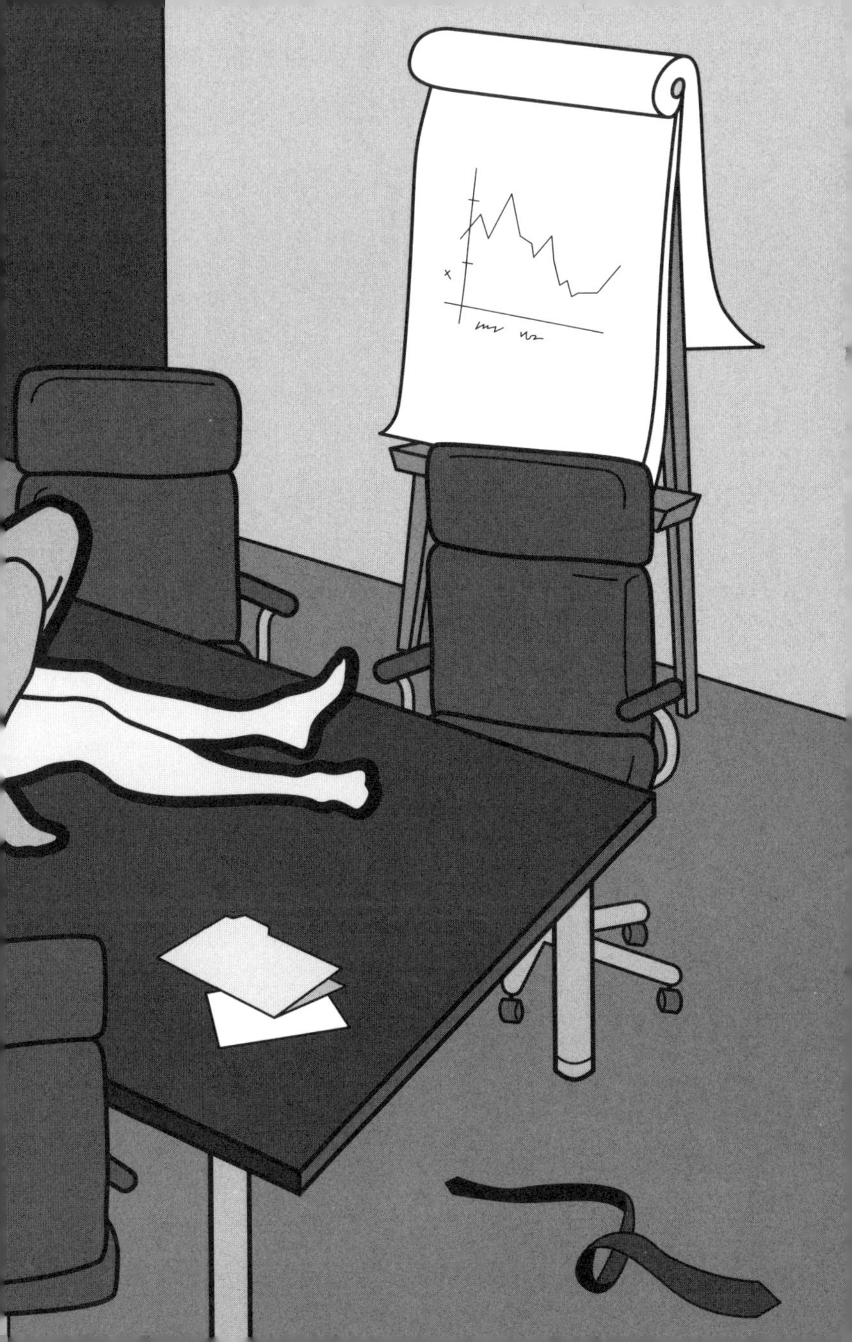

LETTER FROM HAWAII, DECEMBER 16, 2002

by Paul Maliszewski

1310 Hill Street, Apt. A
Durham, NC 27707

December 16, 2002

President George W. Bush
The White House
1600 Pennsylvania Avenue NW
Washington, DC 20500

Dear President Bush,

Have you ever been to Hawaii? Nancy and I went there a year or so ago, or what ended up being about a month before the day she told me we had to separate, and for good this time. Nancy had some work to do. She was in telephony at the time, and I'm being honest when I say I barely understood what it was she did. Basically, telephony consists of all the machines we don't see that make telephones work, the switchers and routers and servers in the specially cooled rooms, with the racks and the stacked up lines and those tiny, tightly braided wires. The company Nancy worked for chose her to attend this big annual industry conference, held that year in Honolulu. She was their most productive account representative.

Our flight landed at night. I had the window seat, Nancy was in the middle, and a businessman with a laptop computer opened on his tray table anchored the aisle. In the air, looking out the window, I couldn't tell where the water ended and the land began. The businessman had scarfed down his meal—pasta primavera and a garden salad—downed a cupful of red wine and then fallen asleep. Brightly colored cartoon fish swam onto and off his computer screen. Whenever they bumped into one another, their lips moved, as if in speech, and strings of bubbles rose to the top of the screen. The plane was dark other than his fish and the strips of white lights illuminating the aisle. A flight attendant came by and gently woke the businessman, asking him to turn off his computer and please store it underneath the seat in front of him. He grunted, looked around, confused, terrified by the sudden proximity of so many strangers, and then complied. Nancy had her eyes shut, but she wasn't sleeping. I looked back out the window again but would be lying if I said I could discern any island from the ocean. There was nothing out there. It was dark and then it was dark and then, maybe a few minutes later, I saw lights. It was the runway—two lines of blue lights and, off to the side, on the other runway, two lines of orange lights. We were in Honolulu.

At the hotel, other people's children pooled around the registration desk as we were checking in and got our room assignment. Some younger kids ran around a couple of ficus trees and hid under the armchairs. Others played tag and did chin-ups on the handrails. We were all getting in late, on the last flight. The desk was understaffed, and the lights in the lobby were dim, almost romantic in a way. The kids were all keyed up though, ready to go. Some of the other guests rode the elevator up with us, getting off here and there. We had a long ride. We made polite conversation on the order of whether this was or was not our first trip to Hawaii. We were staying on the top floor. Two couples got off with us, and we said good night to them as if we were old friends who had together survived some ordeal.

Nancy got right into her pajamas and lay in bed, under the covers, a little out of sorts, I guess. She felt stressed, she said. I ran some warm water on a washcloth, folded it like a blindfold, and placed it over her eyes. She liked that, she said. She held my hand and tightened her grip and then, slowly, relaxed. While she rested I went out for some ice. I walked down the hall and hung a left, tapping the side of my leg with the empty ice bucket as I went. A woman came out of her room with her ice bucket, and we wandered the halls together. Neither of us knew where to find the ice machine. The hotel was massive, with multiple wings, each built like stairs set on their side and connected together by glassed-in walkways that overlooked the ocean and the sky above it and the empty beach below. All the hallways looked identical. We couldn't tell where we had been or which ways we'd already checked. The woman said she was from Ohio.

The next morning Nancy and I carried our complimentary coffees out of the hotel lobby and walked down to the beach. The sun and the tide were both low. I thought of the sun as still at eye-level. It was just starting to warm the water. A couple of dozen people were already at the beach, to beat the midday rush. They planted their umbrellas and spread out their large blankets, staking out private lots of space and shade. I recognized some families and couples from the night before. The woman with the ice bucket was with her husband. They were wading into the water, their bodies seizing up, not yet acclimated to the temperature. Nancy stared at the surf, and I brushed my hand across her cheek, pulling a few strands of hair out of her mouth. We had no place in particular to go until that evening, when Nancy had arranged to meet this vendor for dinner back at the hotel.

"Where to?" I asked.

Nancy shrugged and just pointed in a direction. Left or right, it seemed hardly to matter. Her choice was random. It made no difference. I followed her.

The beach was a thin spit of extra-fine sand followed by a house-sized stretch of black volcanic rock. The rocks were sharp and rough, and the going there was not easy. So we picked our way down the beach, away from the hotel, pausing every now and then to switch from our shoes to our bare soles and then back to our shoes, and so on. The palm trees, tall and skinny to the point of looking starved for water, grew straight up for thirty or forty feet or so and then bent over. Some leaned into one another as drunk companions will when trying to find their way home. Others slouched, their tops nodding toward the sand, like teenagers bored with the same view of the ocean day after day.

After some time, the water turned gray and choppy, and the wind, previously a light, comfortable breeze, became blustery with powerful gusts. Sand blew into my mouth, and as a reflex, I closed my eyes. I turned toward Nancy and, shouting so she could hear me, said, "There may be a storm coming on." As soon as I spoke, big drops of rain started pelting the sand.

Nancy said, "You think?"

Seconds later, the clouds emptied themselves on us, and we ran away from the ocean and took cover underneath the nearest building. When the rain let up, or seemed to, for just a bit, we darted to another building. Then the rain pinned us down again, and we waited. We went block by block like that, scouting ahead through the downpour for dry breezeways and generous overhanging eaves. After about an hour we seemed no nearer to our hotel.

Nancy said, "I'm tired."

"I'm tired, too," I said.

We were standing in front of some local history museum, and the rain was still coming down pretty hard. For lack of anything better to do, we went inside.

Nancy took in an exhibit on native textiles, and I became engaged with another, which unfolded the story, previously unknown to me, of King Kamehameha II and his wife, Queen Kamamalu, and their fateful trip to England, in 1824.

The king was new, and he sought to distinguish himself from his father, who ruled according to tradition. The new king was also young, at twenty-four, and so he thought boldly. His wife was eighteen. He wanted to make Hawaii more like Europe, though he had never visited there. At a feast in celebration of his coronation he defied the ancient taboo that prohibited women from eating with men, or even tasting certain foods, rich, cooked meats, for example. When the chef and his servants entered the king's eating-house and presented the meal to the king and his tribal leaders, the king ordered them to take the best food—the choicest meats and the more delicate dishes—to the queen and the rest of the women. The women had been preparing to eat in a separate house, some distance away. The chef and his servants lingered, unsure whether to obey this order. The king got up from his chair, came around the table, and approached the first servant. He took the platter of meat from the servant's hands and turned to walk in the direction of the women's eating-house. The rest of the servants and the chef followed him. The tribal leaders, after some uncertainty, grumbling, and with not a little discussion, followed as well.

The next year, at the encouragement of several British missionaries, the king and his court began writing letters to each other. Previously, they had relied on messengers and oral instructions. The king and queen began corresponding as well, though they saw each other every day and every night. The king wrote, "Formerly you could only communicate by messenger, who often forgot what you told them to say or else divulged what you trusted them never to reveal. Now, at whatever distance you might be from your friend, you may whisper in his ear."

A museum guard was standing beside a portrait of the king painted shortly after his coronation. The guard was wearing dark gray slacks and a blue blazer. His hands were folded behind him and he was rocking back and forth on his heels. He was listening to music on some earphones. A button on his chest read, "Ask Me." His eyes were closed and his head was bowed and bouncing, keeping time.

In the painting, the king looked like a boy dressed in an older man's costume, a feathered robe and a feathered helmet. His face was full of pride, but it seemed a new look for him, unfamiliar, as if he was trying gainfully to hold the look there, freezing it, while stifling a laugh and the memory of a good joke recently told him. I asked the museum guard if any of the king's letters to his queen were available for viewing.

"What's that, man?" he said. He removed one of the earphones, holding it away from his head. I heard fast, tinny sounds, like frying crickets.

I pointed to the sign I had been reading, that we were both standing beside, and asked again about the letters, if I could see any of them.

"I don't know," he said. "We mostly have these paintings." He motioned behind him at the painting I had been looking at and then replaced his earphone and checked the fit on the other.

"It's a fascinating story," I said.

"What's that?" the guard said. He removed both of his earphones then and let them dangle in front of him, against his chest. I heard the crickets for a second, and then the guard shut them off.

"I never heard of this king and queen before," I said.

The guard nodded.

"It must be old news to you, right?"

The guard looked at the sign and then back at me. "I don't pay these signs much mind," he said.

I nodded and shifted a few steps to my left, to the next painting, and started to read the sign.

"I'm in school to be a dentist," the guard said. He replaced his earphones and checked the fit on both sides. I heard the crickets again, faintly, and then the guard spoke once more, louder this time. "I have to read a lot of stuff about teeth," he said.

The king was curious about the laws and government of England, and had been since first learning about them as a boy, from his tutor, a British-born biologist who visited Hawaii in the company of a scientific voyage and then alienated his captain by showing him up with one too many displays of his knowledge at one too many social events. As a result, the captain and his crew left shortly thereafter, when their stores began to run low, and the biologist came to settle and live alone in Hawaii, learning the language and then the customs of the people and, eventually, ingratiating himself to the old king.

His student, when he became king, decided he wanted to visit England for himself. The trip sounded hazardous and even unnecessary, but though several trusted advisors and his old tutor asked him to reconsider, sending instead an advance party of his choosing, to report back to him in time, none questioned his final decision. The king would take his queen and a number of tribal leaders and attendants with him, and they would all sail on board the next available English whaling ship.

Their accommodations on the ship were far from lavish, but the trip itself was uneventful. On May 21, they landed at Portsmouth to no fanfare. No one was present to greet them. No trumpeters or bands or dignitaries heralded their arrival. No emissary introduced himself and promised to see to their lodging and comfort. The captain, it seemed, hadn't informed his government when they were to arrive.

Someone, a functionary of a functionary of a midlevel official, finally arranged to provide transport for them to London and, from there, showed them to a small hotel and then began to organize an itinerary of events: a trip to Westminster Abbey, visits to factories and breweries and farms, an appointment to see and meet with the children staying in Chelsea hospital, a day at the Epsom races, where the horses were so fast they were said to fly, and then a night of theater at Covent Garden, in the king's box, specially decorated, their hosts hoped, to suit and please their guests' tastes. The royal visitors asked for an audience with the English king, George IV, but were told that he would not be available to meet with them. Newspapers of the day reported on the Hawaiians' every appearance, however mundane the actual details. One article related what the royal visitors ate (fish, poultry, and fresh fruit), noting with approval that they "did not eat to excess, and preferred to drink cider." Another article, published shortly after their arrival, reported on the activities of the queen and her main attendant Liliah:

> When the ladies were seen in London they were dressed in very strange habiliments. The queen wore trousers and a long bedgown of coloured velveteen, and her friend had on something of the same kind. They were playing whist with a pack of very dirty cards, complaining of the cold, and removed from royal dignity.

In no time, all the royal visitors began to dress more in the fashion of Europeans, "in coats by a London tailor and gowns from Paris," and, similarly, one newspaper reporter took note of the growing admiration among the English for the visitors' striking fashions, reporting that "more than one lady begged to have the pattern of the queen's turban."

A family with two children, a boy and a girl, entered the gallery and made as if to walk through it rather quickly. The boy, tall for his age and lanky, trailed behind them all, a few steps back, playing a videogame and humming absently. The family was looking for something else. The mother had a museum pamphlet, opened to the floorplan, and was turning it in every direction, first right-side up and then upside-down, and so on.

"Where are we?" she said. She looked around at the walls and then back down at the map and frowned.

The father stopped before one of the few portraits of the king and queen together and adjusted the straps of his backpack, shifting the load higher onto his shoulders. The mother came over to help, and the girl, older than the boy but not by much, turned the backside of her left hand toward her brother and then got his attention. As he watched her hand, waiting, she moved her other hand up the concealed side, as if it was laboring to climb to the top of a tall wall. After a few seconds, just when it appeared her brother was about to lose interest and return his attention to his videogame, his sister's middle finger rose above the other hand. She laughed and then revealed her whole hand to him. Her brother rushed at her and pushed her to the floor. There was a scuffle and then a cry. The mother and father yelled at their son in hushed tones, letting their angry, distended faces do the work of louder voices. The father rushed over to help his daughter up. She indicated she was okay, that it was no big deal, and then made a point of starting to walk with a slight limp and an outrageously pained grimace on her face. The family turned around and left through the door they entered.

The king and his company were returning one afternoon from a tour of a millinery shop, where they all purchased at least one hat, when they passed a fish seller and his cart. One of the tribal leaders saw, at the back of the cart, on top of a heap of other fish, a great fish, larger by far than all the rest, measuring at least four feet in length and weighing as much as a good-sized child, and maybe more. The tribal leader pointed at the fish and asked their British minder what it was.

"Mullet," he said. "That's a grey mullet." The fish was not to his liking, personally.

The tribal leader got his king's attention, and the king, after examining the mullet, indicated it to the queen. Liliah, the queen's main attendant, stepped forward to examine the mullet and then nodded her approval to the queen, who in turn nodded her approval to the king, who then asked the minder if they had money enough to acquire the fish. The minder demurred that they, of course, had plenty of money, but that he felt obligated to remind the king that they could all enjoy far more delicious fish, prepared to their liking, at a restaurant tonight.

The king, however, wanted this fish.

"It's a fish from our native sea," he said. "We catch mullet. It's a good fish."

The minder negotiated quickly with the owner of the fish cart, who began to wrap the fish in yesterday's newspaper.

The king said, "I find it hard to believe this fish didn't swim here just for us."

Two of the king's attendants took the wrapped mullet from the fish seller, nodded their heads in thanks, and carried the package back to the hotel.

On June 10, one of the king's closest attendants fell ill. The royal party cancelled their scheduled good will trip to a prison. On the next day, several more of the attendants became sick, and on the following day, rather late in the afternoon, a doctor was summoned to the hotel. He examined the royal visitors and declared them stricken with measles. On June 13, the king and queen, previously well and displaying no symptoms, became very ill. Over the next week, nearly all of the tribal leaders and attendants became sick. No Hawaiian in history had ever caught a case of measles, sir. They had no natural immunity against the disease.

For the next month, the royal party remained confined to their hotel rooms. The king and queen slept apart, on separate floors, their attendants and a few doctors around them. A few of their number became better, and then a few died. On the morning of July 8, Liliah told the king's main attendant that several doctors had just determined that the queen was not likely to recover. The king, upon hearing the news, asked to be placed in his armchair and carried to the queen's room.

The king greeted his wife as the attendants carried him into her room. The queen asked the king to go away please. He did not go away. Instead he asked his attendants to lift him onto her bed, and so they picked him up by his arms, which had shrunk and withered to a fraction of their former size, and placed him on the queen's bed, by her side. The queen asked the king not to look at her. He embraced her instead and then he wept, and when he remembered that they were not alone, he asked his attendants to leave and wait outside the room.

In the evening, he called to his attendants and asked to be put in his armchair again and carried back to his room. An hour later, the queen, his wife, was dead.

The king's health deteriorated rapidly. He was never not coughing. His attendants did not believe he slept. His spirits sank, and he expressed the wish, to anyone who would listen and every doctor who arrived to attend to and try to cure him, not to survive his wife.

Early in the morning of July 14, his attendants awoke to the sound of the king's voice. The king was speaking. They could hear him through the door. Perhaps he was dictating a letter or communicating with his doctor. They entered his room, believing, hoping really, that his health had improved in the night. The king was in his bed, and the curtains on the bed were drawn. Inside, the king was speaking, as clearly as he spoke when healthy. "I am dying," he said. "I am dying." He continued to pronounce himself as dying until his prediction became true.

Nancy came up behind me while I was reading about the royal visitors in mourning, how the women, adopting European customs, purchased black silk dresses that brushed the ground when they walked and black hats with long veils, and how all the survivors made the long trip home, across the Atlantic Ocean again, around South America, and back to Hawaii.

"There you are," Nancy said. She walked up and stood beside me and looked for a second at a contemporary artist's conception of the king's agony over the loss of his wife. It was all very abstract, dark colors and thick swirls from a heavy brush.

"How were the textiles?" I asked.

"Very textiley," Nancy said. "I don't know, they were just textiles. Pretty enough, I guess."

I pointed to the canvas in front of us. "This is all about this Hawaiian king mourning his dead wife," I said.

Nancy looked again and nodded.

I said, "When the king was told of his wife's death, he told the people around him—and this is a quote—'I feel within as if all is not right.' And as he said that to them, he gripped his stomach." I gripped my stomach with both my arms. "Like this," I said.

"His stomach hurt him?" Nancy said.

"No," I said. "He meant his feelings were not all right. His feelings were in his stomach. Hawaiians apparently—I got this from one of these signs—think of their stomachs as the place where all their feelings come from. You know, like how we talk about our feelings and our hearts."

Nancy turned to look behind us, at all the paintings and signs I'd read before coming here, to this.

"Isn't that weird?" I said. "Their belly is our heart."

"What did he die of?" Nancy asked.

"Measles," I said. "A bunch of them caught measles and died."

"I think it's getting late," Nancy said. "We should be getting back to the hotel."

"They'd never been to England," I said. "They'd never been anywhere but Hawaii, and then they went and took this long trip to England, and they just died."

"I took a long trip by the entrance on my over," Nancy said. "It looks like it's stopped raining."

"This was a long time ago," I said.

*

While Nancy went to the bathroom to dress and get ready for her dinner/meeting, I stretched out on the bed and stared at the ceiling. I interlaced my hands behind my head and tried just to relax. My arms and shoulders felt tight, and my feet were sore from the walking. I wiggled my spine and shifted my legs, looking for an ideal arrangement of my limbs and, finally, some comfort. My elbows poked out beside my head like little wings. The ceiling was rough and bumpy, almost mountainous. I imagined it to be the surface of a white planet.

Nancy started yelling, and I went to see what the problem was. She was looking at herself in the mirror, and there was a sound coming out of her, a kind of low, loud growl, that I'd never heard her make before. It was the sound of frustration without end. Her jaw was set. Her hands were clenched, one around her hairbrush and the other balled up in a fist. Her knuckles were turning white.

"What's going on?" I said to her.

"Fucking hair," she said. She was standing on a towel in her underwear and bra. Her hair was out to the tips of her shoulders, frizzy at the ends and in fine knots at the top.

"It's always all so fucking tangled," she said. She hit the side of her hairbrush on the edge of the sink. She struck at the sink nine or ten times. I could hear voices outside our door, milling around and then heading down the hall.

"Let me help," I said. I reached for her brush.

"Here," I said. Her grip tightened around the brush, and she pressed the side of it against the countertop. "Can I help?" I said.

"It won't come untangled," she said. "It just won't."

"What can I do? Can I do something?" I said. "For you."

"I have to be somewhere," she said.

"I know," I said.

"Just leave me alone," she said. "Will you?"

I went back and lay on the bed and listened to Nancy finish with her preparations, to the sounds of clothes going on and zippers, and makeup containers opened and then makeup containers closed. I stared again at the ceiling. I tried to remember where I had been. The ceiling was rough and bumpy, I thought, almost mountainous. I imagined it to be the surface of a white planet, and then I imagined myself to be a very small explorer who was called upon by his patron, a king, and charged with making a map of this new place and returning with reports about whatever I happened to find there. I wandered among the peaks and valleys of plaster. I rounded the bases and crested the tops. I was patient. As an explorer I moved slowly. I'd never been here before. At night I slept in the shadow of a mountain. The next day, I encountered a spider and fought with it for my life. I wondered what I would do once Nancy left for the night, and then I thought I would like very much to continue to do just what I was doing.

Nancy came around the corner and said she was

heading down now.

"You're all ready?" I asked.

She raised her hands from her side, as if presenting herself as ready, and then shrugged. "I guess," she said.

"You got everything?" I said.

"I got my purse," Nancy said, holding up her purse. She didn't need anything else.

"Well, you look great," I said. She was wearing her suit. I always liked when she wore her suit.

Nancy thanked me, and I followed her to the door. While she undid the lock, I hugged her from behind and smelled her neck.

"Good luck," I said.

"Thanks," Nancy said.

"You're beautiful," I said.

"Thanks," she said.

"You look great," I said.

"You're real sweet."

"I'll see you when you get back," I said. "Okay?"

Nancy told me I didn't have to wait up, that she might be late.

"I don't mind," I said. I followed her into the hall and leaned out toward her, propping the door open with my foot, so I wouldn't get locked out.

"I might be late," she said and headed down the hall away from me.

That night there was another storm. I was lying in bed on my back, sort of just staring at the ceiling and sort of thinking about what it must have been like when the survivors of the royal party returned to Hawaii. Dozens of long boats, manned by the strongest rowers from the islands, came out to greet them. Fishermen abandoned their work, dropping their nets and spears, and rushed to be at the side of the English ship as it approached. Representatives of all the tribes rowed out as well. The English ship dropped its anchor, and the islanders' boats pulled alongside. They hailed their return. They cheered. Their stomachs, I imagine, felt within as if all was right, full with good feeling. People without boats swam out to meet the returning party as well. They bobbed in the water by the sides of the boats and shouted up their hellos. It was then that they learned that their king and queen had died.

The storm was a bad one, and it would not relent. I turned off the lights in our room, opened the curtains wide, and went back to lay on the bed. Lightning flashed and lit the room and me inside it. The storm surrounded the hotel, and thunder shook the walls. Rain splashed against the windows in thick sheets, and lightning flashed again. I saw the bolt this time. It raced out of the sky, emerging from the clouds, and headed down toward the ocean, before forking wildly in three directions. I turned away from the window, and the lightning was there, imprinted on my eyes or marked on my brain. I closed my eyes and saw the bolt and the three forks still. A storm like this could surround the whole island. It could contain us all. I felt like the last lone shrimp stuck on the end of a skewer. This collection of islands, these mountains, volcanoes, and waterfalls, these rocks which had been covered by ocean and then rose out of it, could just as soon sink back into it.

I got up from the bed and went into the hallway to see if anyone else was here with me. It was deserted. I came back inside, grabbed the keycard and the ice bucket, and left to look around.

I was not wandering long before I ran into the woman with the ice bucket again. She was with her husband and she had her hand on his arm as they walked. They were supporting each other. She was shorter than he; in heels she came up just about to his chest. She was leaning into him, and he was leaning into her.

"You need more ice?" the woman said. She said it as if I was being wasteful with the stuff.

She turned to her husband and explained about how she'd run into me the night before.

"The man likes his ice," the husband said.

"I guess I do go through a lot of ice," I said.

The husband said, "Do these people know how to make a mixed drink or what?"

"We were at the bar downstairs," the woman explained. "It's a nice bar."

"It's a really nice bar," the husband said. "They've got plenty of ice."

We spoke then of the weather, the terrible storms,

the rain, and the thunder.

"You know," the husband said, "we should all get to know one another better." He looked at the top of his wife's head.

"We really should," the woman said.

As soon as we exchanged names and shook hands and traded room numbers and then promised to make plans—soon, maybe tomorrow, if you have time—to get together and have drinks or perhaps dinner, I knew that we never would. I said good night to the couple and continued down the hallway. They went into their room, and I heard the door lock behind them, the snick of the deadbolt and then the short length of chain falling against the door. I doubled back, deciding I never needed ice anyway and soon was in our room again, in bed, watching the rest of the storm.

Today, at the museum, I learned a curious thing, sir. One account of the return of the royal party tells of how Liliah, the queen's main attendant, left the main deck of the English ship and retreated back into her cabin when her countrymen drew near and started to call out. The sign I read at the museum made much of how and why Liliah left. The sign suggested that living even briefly in the company of Europeans had made her feel embarrassed and maybe even ashamed at the sight of the swimmers and the rowers and the tribesmen, all of whom were mostly naked. Liliah, the sign explained, was made newly modest by travel and her experience with another culture. She was, in effect, like a European. I had my doubts. Is it not possible, I wondered, that Liliah was embarrassed by something else? Could she not have retreated for some other reason? If she indeed felt shame—and I suspect she did—could it not have been because she thought she had failed? The woman who had been in her care was gone. The queen was dead. Liliah had departed the island on a ship with their king and their queen. She returned, five months later, on another ship, with no king and no queen. Bodies of naked swimmers would, I wager, be no great shock at all.

Keep up the good work, sir.

Sincerely,

Harvey Strub

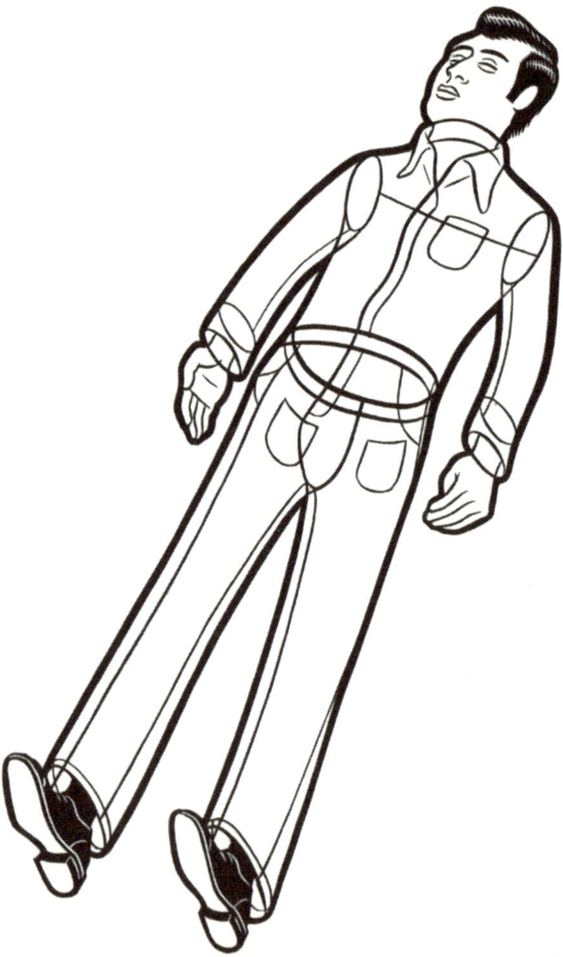

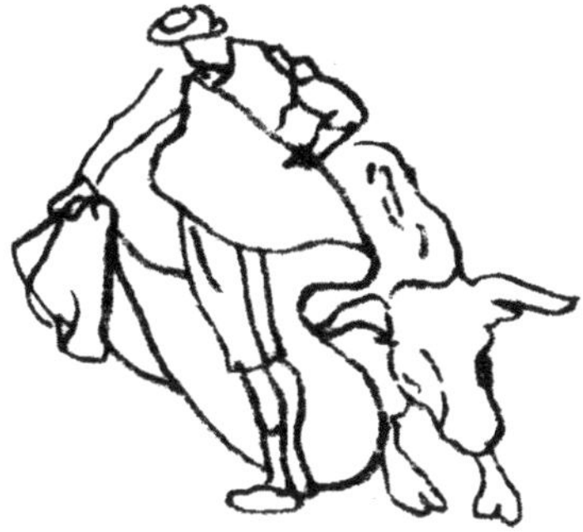

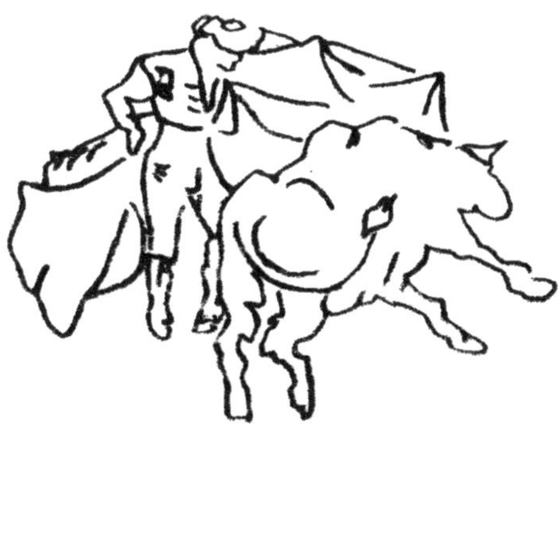

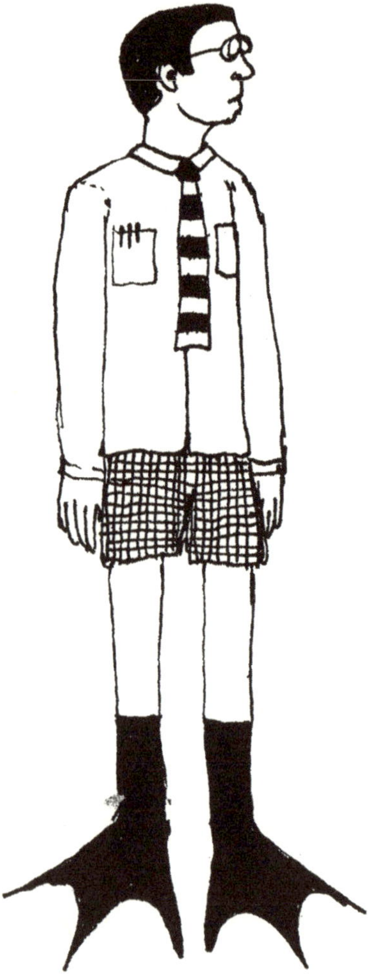

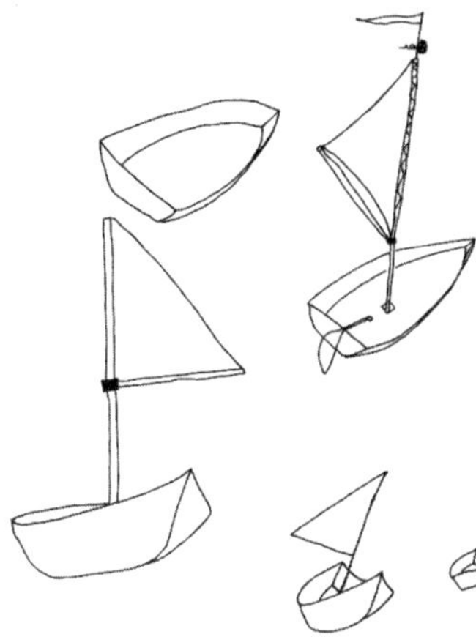

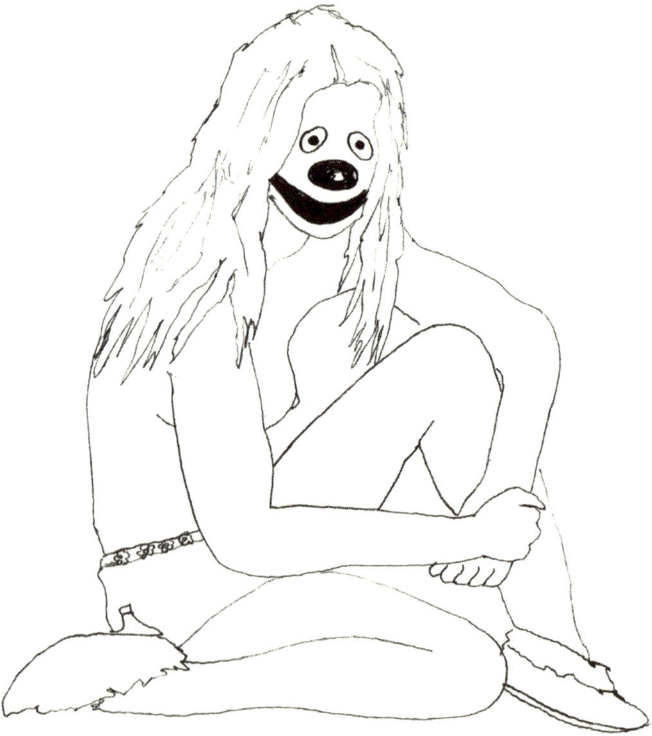

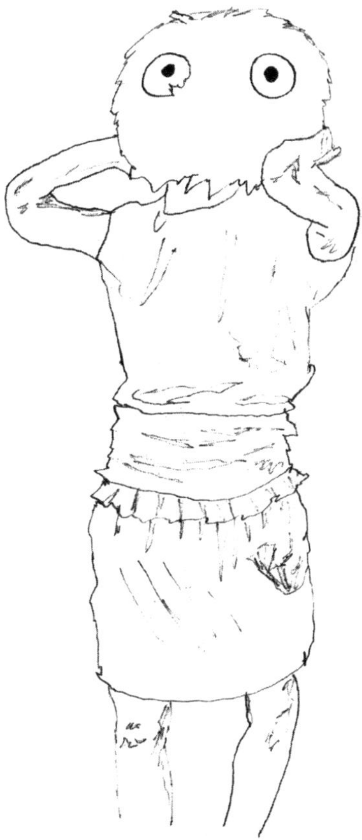

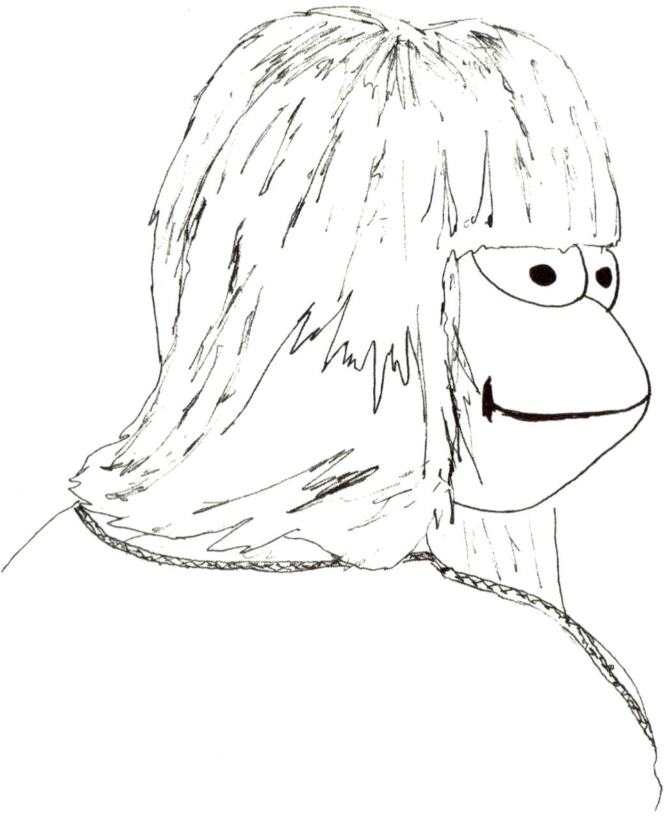

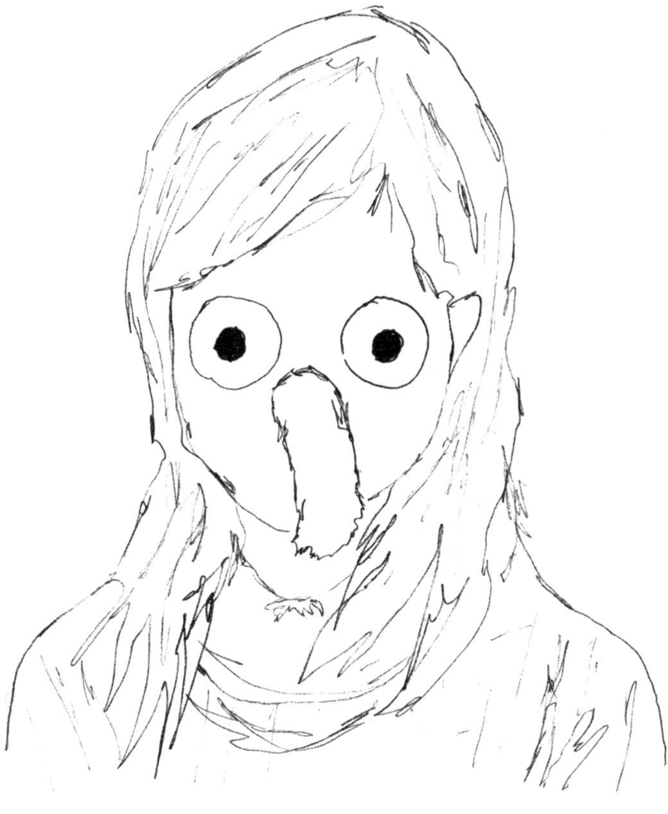

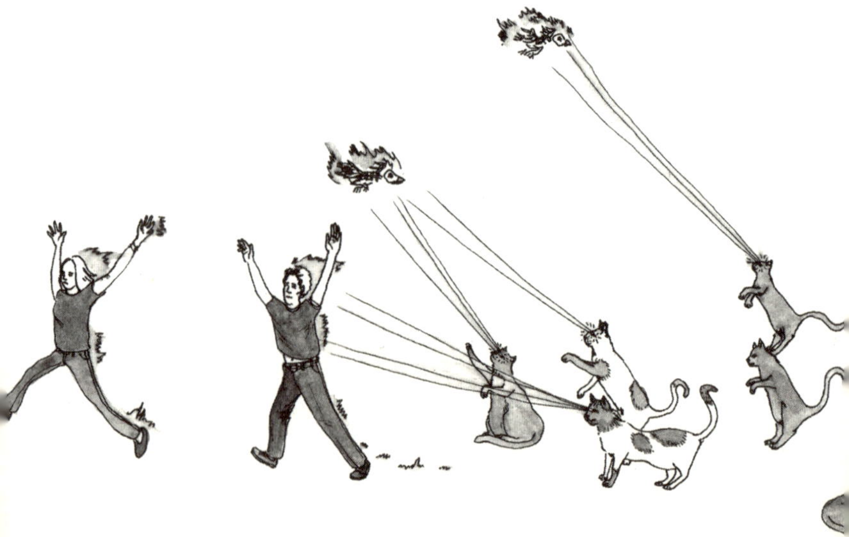

Under his imperfect knot, the one he's holding out to me for inspection, I can see his leg muscles slowly shift as he moves in his hiking boots. There's light blonde hair down the calves, darker hair on the shins. There's a scab on his knee from the fall on Day 1 of the hike. I pass the knot back to him. He's forgotten to trim the loose ends. Still, I tell him it's wonderful, perfect, and stick a star on his shirt with my thumb.

They take walks between the driftwood logs and return with hands full of water washed glass and thin shells. In a blue hankerchief I've set out on the beach we wrap up the ones that we agree are wonderful, and that tell us something about what water does to rock over time. I pass around his smooth, oval stone and each set of small hands holds onto it for a moment. At noon they gather around the tidepool with their heads bowed. The circle of their blonde necks, each one slick with sunscreen, hides the water from my view. But I already know exactly which starfish and barnacles and anemones are there.

BOY SCOUT LEADER

by Sarah Shawn

The tidepool teems with life, I tell them. It's life layered upon life. Each of the elements gives way to another.

Do the bears eat life in a tidepool, he asks.

No. The bears eat salmon in the river.

After lunch I open a black plastic bag and walk around to each of them. They deposit their garbage. He doesn't look at me, doesn't acknowledge me, just drops his drinking box in. We hike inland.

My flashlight beam hits the flies of their tents and then it rolls over the insides. I can see comic books, unwashed clothes, unwashed sleeping bags, velcro wallets.

He comes into my tent at nine fifteen, an hour after lights out. My toothbrush is still in the tin cup. The toothpaste, rolled halfway, is beside it. My sleeping bag is still rolled. My pillow is rolled. I know what this is about. We sing songs when we walk the trails and blow whistles to keep the bears away. Every night I hoist our food up into a tree while the scouts hit metal tent stakes into the ground. But still, some are scared. Every shift of a fern is a claw. Today, after lunch, when we passed the falls, he sat down on the trail and began to cry. Dark moss on the side of a tree was a bear. The other scouts stood away from him, kicked mulch off the walkway and waited. It's nothing but moss, I told him. I took his hand.

What's this on your hand?

I had to wipe my nose, he said.

I put his hand on the moss and held it there.

It's not a bear. It's only moss you think is in the shape of a bear.

He nodded his head.

Tell me what it is?

His fingers flexed beneath mine.

It's moss.

He's crying now in the dark and wiping his nose with his hand. I tell him to stop. I adjust the lantern and his legs emerge in the light. The blackberry scratches, the goosebumps, the thin line of black trim at the bottom of his scout shorts. Outside the river water continues to pass us. The invisible movement in the forest continues. We've talked about the sounds of the raccoons, the deer, and the other animals that use the cover of night to find food, but amongst themselves they talk about death at the hands of a bear.

Our food is in a tree I tell him.

I know.

The bears are as afraid of us as we are of them.

I know.

Don't wipe your nose.

I can't help it.

Here.

I tear off four squares. I carry all the toilet paper. It lets me know where they are at all times. With this one I walk out into the woods to make sure there are no bears. When we reach a clearing far enough from the campsite he pulls his pants down.

You don't have to look, he says.

When he's finished, he asks for paper and I unroll four squares and rip the perforations. Some of them don't even ask. Some go into the bush and wipe with leaves. I'm trying to run a clean camp.

He wipes his nose. The black flies roll off the tent and their shadows disappear. I hang the lantern from a clip on one of the poles and its light swings for a moment, making shadows grow large and then thin. He's wiped his eyes with the four squares of toilet paper, so he hands them back and I put them down next to the tin cup.

I'm not having fun, he says.

I unroll four more squares and rip the perforations.

When the food is lowered it is wet with dew. They rest drinking boxes on their knees. I shake out 225ml of granola for each and mix the powdered milk. Their legs are dirtier today; the dry dust of the campsite has lifted and settled on them. I work the sunscreen into their necks. Slowly, but they know it takes time. He asks me if there are some smells that attract bears.

No.

Are you sure?

I slip my hand under the neckband of his shirt and rub into his shoulderblades, then over and across his collarbone and the top of his chest.

I'm sure.

I think I can do my own arms, he says.

Don't anyone make a sound, I tell them, but two are talking so the woodpecker leaves its perch and disappears into the pines. I look back at their single file line. Everyone is wearing a hat. Everyone has a whistle around his neck.

Do we want to see birds?

No one speaks.

Wasn't one of our goals before we left to see birds?

Yes, he says, halfway down the line.

Then next time I ask for silence, I would like silence.

I hoist food up into the tree. The scouts hit tent stakes into the ground. If everyone doesn't sing, it's not worth it, I tell them while the campfire burns. The logs are erupting.

Each scout can throw in one stick.

Get your sticks and make sure they are not too large, I tell them. Each one can throw in one stick but only when I say it is their turn.

The scouts get up and disappear from the orange light of the flames one by one. They return with one piece of wood each, some carrying logs covered in woodbugs that crawl across their fingers. Others carry splintered, green limbs of pine. He gets up. It's his turn. I can see him through the flames.

I want you to come with me, he says.

One of the other scouts throws his log in the fire.

Why?

I don't want to be attacked by a bear.

We pass four good sticks but he walks further, his

hand holding on to my pointer, middle, and ring fingers. The fire behind us makes the wet ferns blink orange. He stops next to a stump.

I didn't bring any paper with me, I say to him after he's lowered his shorts.

The food is gone in the morning. The frayed rope hangs above what remains of the juice boxes. All but two have been crushed by something heavy. The sandwiches have been flipped over and left untouched. The cylinder of peanut butter is gone. Tubes of jam are ripped.

It's just jam, I tell them. It's not blood. No one's injured. The bear is gone.

When they've stopped crying I collapse each of their tents.

That's why we put food in a tree away from the camp, I tell them, but they continue to cry, wiping tears from their eyes.

When we finally make it back, the parents are leaning against their cars and against the ranger's truck. The policeman is talking to a father. When we walk on to the pavement, the mothers come running across to grab their children. I don't see his mother's face. Her blonde hair is covering it. She's rubbing his back hard, asking him the same question again and again.

What happened to you? What happened to you?

He's crying.

The police officer is walking towards me.

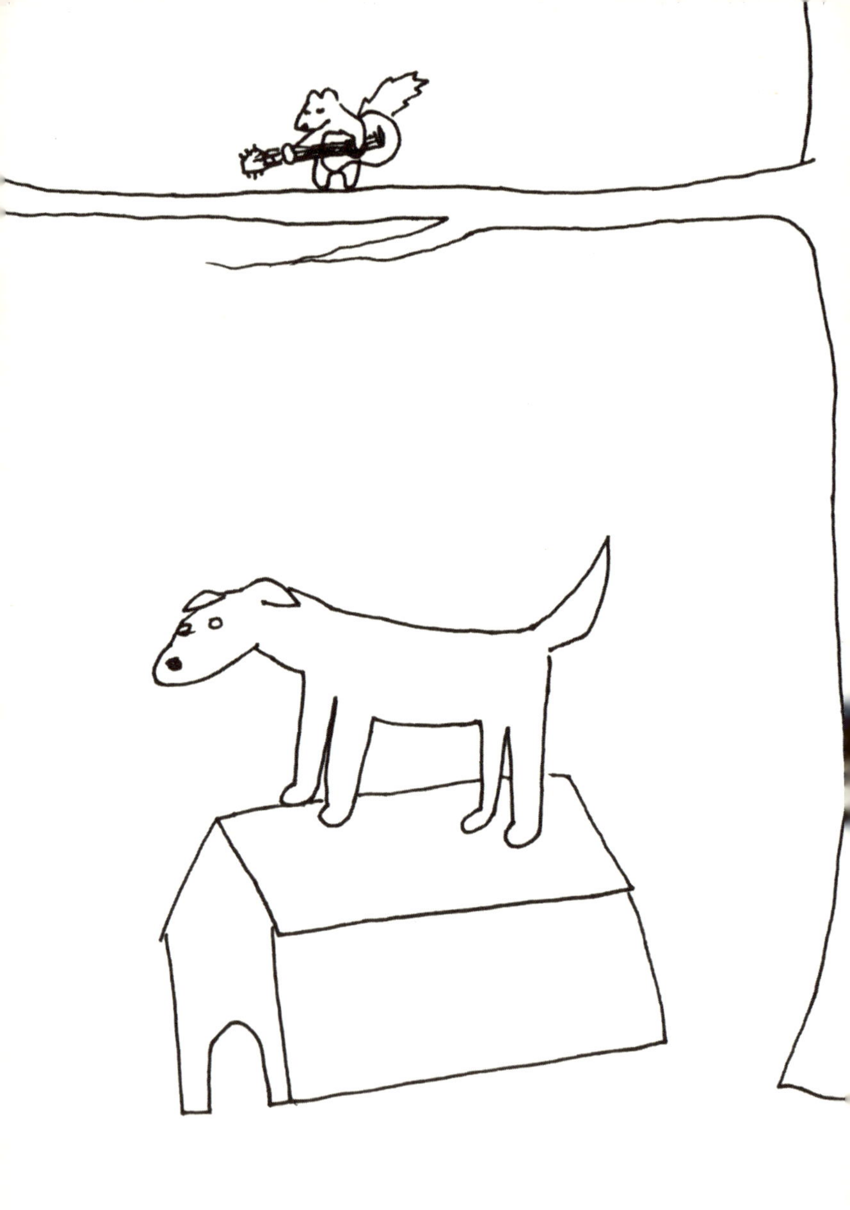

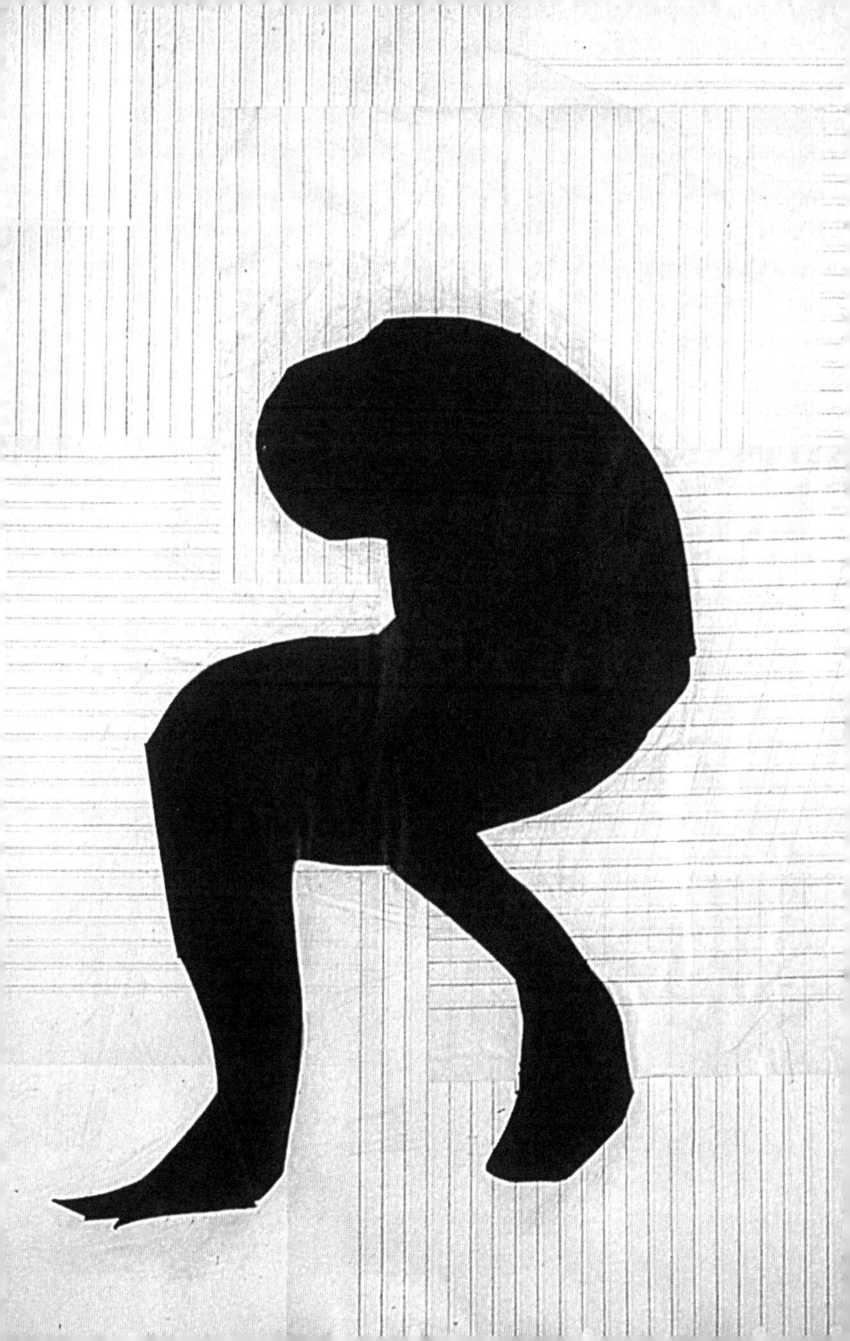

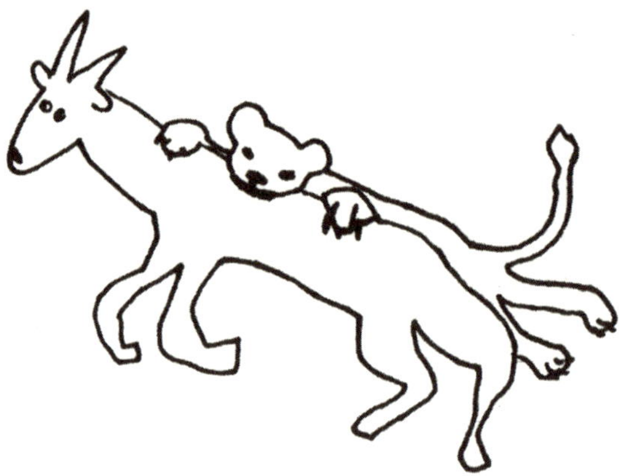

Ee-ay, Oh-oh, and Ah-ee, which I understand their names to be, try to assure me in their finest English that I'm not to worry about the dead boy in the puddle.

Ee-ay: "It's normal Habana."

Ah-ee: "Jus' a fucking crackhead, mange."

Oh-oh: "I speak-a for you: Now is the time for walking."

Me: "Yes, walking."

Walking away. Not at the slow Cuban saunter, where all the hot street is taken up through the nose, all the chicas appraised, but back at my speed, firm and direct: big city. The speed you would imagine walking away from the site of a dead boy lying in a puddle of sewage on a fractured cobblestone street with his eyes open but glazed frosty white. Open but closed.

I keep this pace for several blocks and when I turn, my three friends are gone. They reappear from around a corner. They retain swagger. In Centro, this warm, corroded neighbourhood where I'm staying, the retention of swagger seems indomitable and molten. A magma of swagger: It is solid and fluid. The warmth is friendly; the heat is mean.

HABANA

by Corey Keegan

We move together to the Paseo Marti, a wide boulevard divided by twin rows of trees flanking an open promenade paved with polished granite. The whole plaza is watched by unsmiling police in mirrored sunglasses at their posts among the people: thatched lovers, prostitutes on the arms of tourists attempting dignity. Mostly old men, with young women, but there are old women with young men, old men with muscled young men, old men with unmuscled young men. And perched on the concrete benches that face away from the grinding old cars and horns in the street are the compatriots of Ee-ay, Oh-oh, and Ah-ee. They all get the thumbs up, the high five, the low five.

Ee-ay: "In Habana, evrybody frens."

Ah-ee: "Evrybody da fucking frens."

Oh-oh: "I a speak-a for you. You is frens."

Me: "Yes, we're all friends, aren't we."

We are whistled over by a police officer. I'd read in an appendix to my phrase book that this was routine. The police request identification, whisper in their radios from under square, black mustaches, and generally inconvenience their subjects. This time however, the three are put in a police car with little complaint and I'm left in the shadow of the billowing trees wondering what's just happened as Ee-ay frantically plays for my attention from the backseat. He's pointing me back in the direction from which we had come. And then he is gone.

All three are gone.

Ee-ay, swarthy Spanish, but with yellowed eyes, who dreams of playing Salsa to the crowds of Barcelona.

Ah-ee, black, handsome, smiling, constantly accounting his sexual exploits with female tourists, and confirming he will survive by fucking these vacationers until Cuba is "okay" and he can get a job and buy a Ferrari.

Oh-oh. Mulatto, eyes an Irish green, skin a creamed gold. Quiet and watchful and will, he tells me, play for the New York Yankees someday when he has better shoes.

I have only been here one day. Those boys who were just now arrested introduced themselves to me outside the Hotel Cuba Libra, where I was about to pay fifty American dollars for a room. They offered me an apartment at their house for fifteen. I had expected this to happen. I read about it in my phrase book. The book said it would be safe, so I agreed. But now can I find my way back to the apartment? Can I find my way to the front door from which I emerged earlier, to see a boy lying in a greenish brown puddle on a narrow and fractured cobblestone street, his eyes open and closed, along side of which sat ragged and rusty old men eyeing me with difference and indifference, with hardened magma.

Perhaps I will choose to not find my way back. I can abandon the program. I can give up on my adventurous notion of among-the-people travel. I could become a tourist. I could find a posh hotel with heavy security. But I won't. With greater ease than expected, I return twenty minutes later to my room. The three have already been released and are waiting for me with Ee-ay's parents, cousins, girlfriend, aunts, sisters, and a smudge of grimy children, their ears pierced with golden loops. The adults laugh at my look of concern. The children smack the ground with sticks, this is their game.

Ee-ay: "It's normal Habana." Laughs.

Ah-ee: "Fucking cops, mange, fucking cops." Laughs.

Oh-oh: "You, look at you." Laughs.

Eye-oh, Ee-ay's mother: Laughs.

Oh-Eh-Oh, husband of Eye-oh: Laughs.

Me: "Hilarious."

The noise subsides and preparations are made for a meal with the family. I lock myself in my room to read. The apartment is actually the size of prison cell. A single mattress, a single sheet, a single pillow case stuffed with bits of foam. A shower nozzle which produces small ribbons of neutral water, a toilet with no toilet seat. A cup. A knife. A fork. A plate. A small television.

To colour this tiny confine, the wall at the foot of the bed is carefully arranged with fist-sized stuffed animals, the sort you win on the Midway at an amusement park. On the wall at the head of the bed is a large poster of a blonde woman in a bathing suit, titled Ms. October, 1988. I imagine the normal occupants of the bed, who will sleep next door on the floor until my departure. I imagine them in sex, in a standard missionary position. She holds a concentrated gaze on her stuffed toy collection, symbols of his adoration, the sweet man, the sweet things he does for her. And he above, kisses her deeply, raises his head to gasp, and takes in an inspirational glance at the impossible breasts of Ms. October, 1988.

I read a fast ten or twenty words. Blink. Dead. Sewage. Try not to … Read and concentrate on the words in the book by this dead guy. Dead. Okay fine. I watch the news in Spanish on the tiny TV.

When the meal is ready, there is a knock at my door. I enter the narrow courtyard to enjoy rice and beans, topped with sliced cucumber, fried bananas and avocado. It is all sumptuous, filling and good. I push the plate away, and dispatch Oh-oh to the store with six dollars intended for the purchase of two bottles of rum, three cans of cola and some ice. Minutes later, he returns with all but the ice.

Ee-ay: "Hello. Ice is a hard to get."

Ah-ee: "Fucking."

Oh-oh: "I a speak-a for you: It's OK," and opens a new package of cigarettes and passes them among his friends.

Me: "Yes, OK friends."

The rum and cola is poured, in equal measures, into three glasses, and shared between six people, then seven, then nine, then ten. I field simple questions about Canada. They are interested in how much things cost. A pair of Nikes? A pair of Levi's? A beer? A cigar? A bottle of rum? A Ferrari? And then my job: how much money do I make? How big is my house? How many girlfriends do I have? How many hours do you have to know a Canadian girl before you can fuck her?

"Why you has no fucking Ferrari?"

My answers disappoint, though I'm tempted to

invent, I try to tell only truth. On other journeys, among other strangers, I have crafted long, lavish, and incredible tales, but on this night I cannot lie with these hostile innocents. They would believe anything I told them, they would do so without twitch or glare, suspicion or amazement, only with molten swagger tainted faintly with resentment and reproach.

The night is soft and supple. People appear from the other apartments. People appear from the street. They smile horrific yellow nubby teeth, brightened in contrast to their dark faces. They swag on the bottles. They teach me to Salsa. The men borrow my razor and shave one another's faces. The women show me their breasts. They wash my dirty socks, stitch my broken seams. They fry more bananas and smoke the filterless cigarettes. They bring me a piece of salty ham and give me a haircut. They try to sell me cigars, jewelry, a car, the services of a car, marijuana, cocaine, sex with their daughters, sex with their wives, their sisters, nieces, nephews, brothers, sons. They listen to a story about my girlfriend with dissatisfaction. They finish the food, the cigarettes and the rum. Everything has been shared, and is now gone.

I go to sleep without locking my door. They steal my cash, my traveller's cheques, my camera, my toothpaste.

The next morning, the people of Centro Habana wake. I barely join them. My soggy head is wrapped in a towel, as tourniquet against the slices of white light that gouge my room. The sound of an old transmission buzzes somewhere outside. When I wink out of the window, to the rear of the apartment, my eyes fix on an open-air garage, six legs on the ground protruding from the belly of a rusted, roped-up, stapled-up, bus, which is snorting, and wheezing, and shaking off small flecks of brown rust like some enormous asthmatic dog. Another man is behind the wheel grunting instructions. The noise, the gears grinding, and the smell of gasoline, piled onto my rumhead forces me to the floor, where I will have to decide what to do about last night's theft.

I could go to the cops, which would expedite the refund of the travellers cheques, without which I will be stuck. It would also mean trouble for not only the person or persons who stole my things, but for the family as well. Classic: my wellbeing versus their wellbeing. My being was not well, that was for certain, whereas one of my new friend's being was markedly weller. And of course there was the dead boy, whose open eyes I still see when I close my own. He wasn't even being, and compared to a bed of cobblestone and a pillow of sewage, my trouble is not a great one. Still, I have to decide.

Ee-Eh, Ah-Ee, and Oh-Oh are draped over the courtyard when I open my door in mid afternoon. Would the guilty man make such an appearance? No, but would the guilty man stay away? No, for it would demonstrate his guilt. I search the three for new shoes, new clothes, new sheepish looks of counterfeit innocence. Nothing but cool smiles, the high five, the low five, and the midday magma. I try to explain I'm not interested in their company. I need to make a decision. It doesn't translate. And so we walk to the capitol, the museum, past the new hotels and bars. The indecipherable traffic, a mechanical organism of attempted murder, swerving bleating and careening around us. The colonial facades dropping debris and otherwise dilapidating. The statues of Communists. Posters of Fidel and Che. The sites no longer impress. I am angry. I am handed a warmish coffee, with sweetish sugar, a small paper cone full of roasted peanuts, a glass of fruit juice bought from an old woman in a doorway and shared rectangularly. I am told to pay. I am told to smile.

And as we walk I'm always a moment away from a cop. I am always a moment from telling, from giving out, from dying, becoming a rat, the friend of nobody. I have been robbed.

After a few hours of walking, my hosts are wearing on me. I've taken more money from a bank machine, something the phrase book said would not work. Ee-ay, Oh-oh, and Ah-ee insist on touching the money. Counting the money. They are becoming obsequious.

It is not too much longer before, again, we are whistled over by a police officer. This time though a cop speaks to me directly. He asks where I'm staying.

Me: "With those guys." I point.

Ee-ay: Shakes his head at me. No.

Me: "In a house, over there." I point.

Oh-oh: Smile pinched off, finger over his mouth.

Me: "Where the dead boy was found." I point.

Ah-ee: Stares at his shoes.

Me: "With those guys." I point.

Me: "The dead boy." I point.

Me: "Those guys." I point.

They are handcuffed and put into a car. I turn by back to them. I spin on my heels, 180 degrees. I remove dark sunglasses from my pocket, slide them over my eyes, and I go back to where I was before.

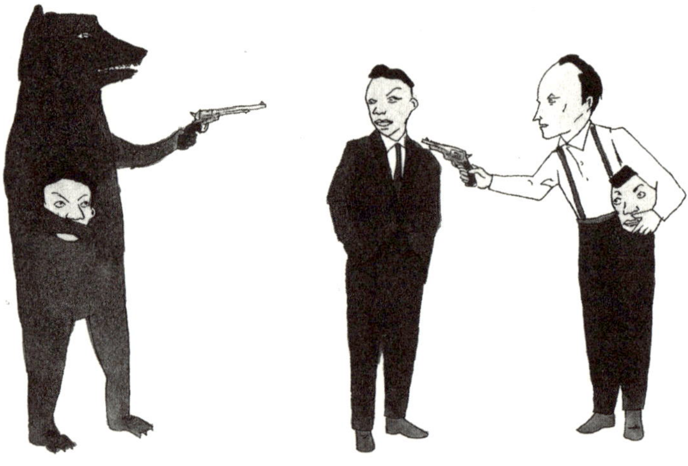

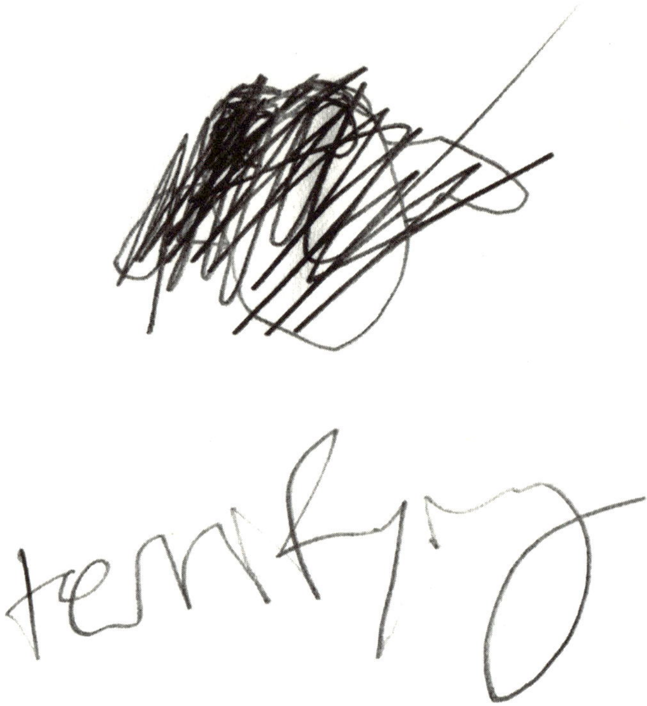

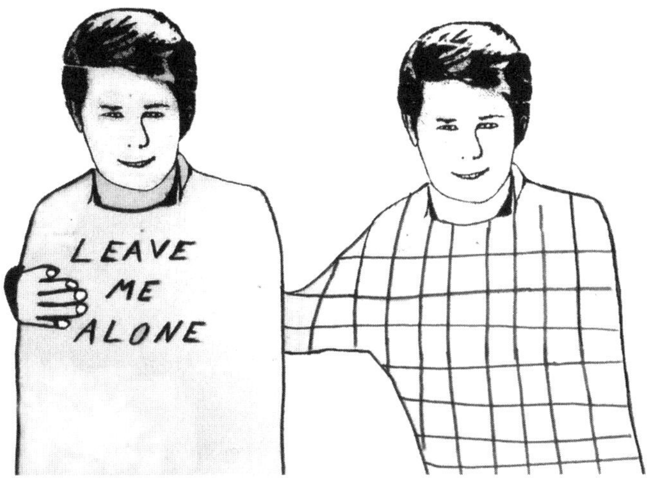
LEAVE
ME
ALONE

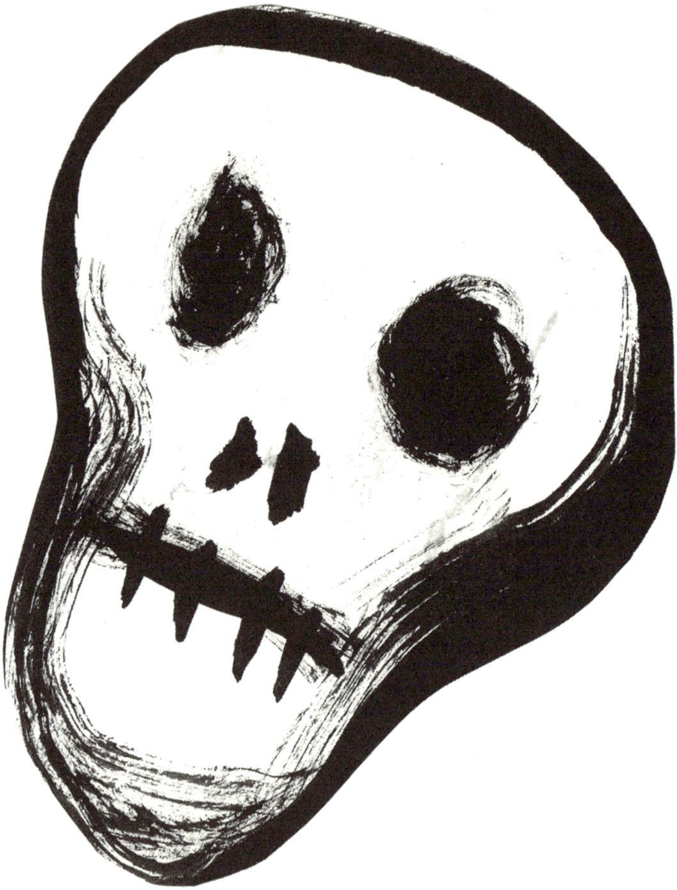

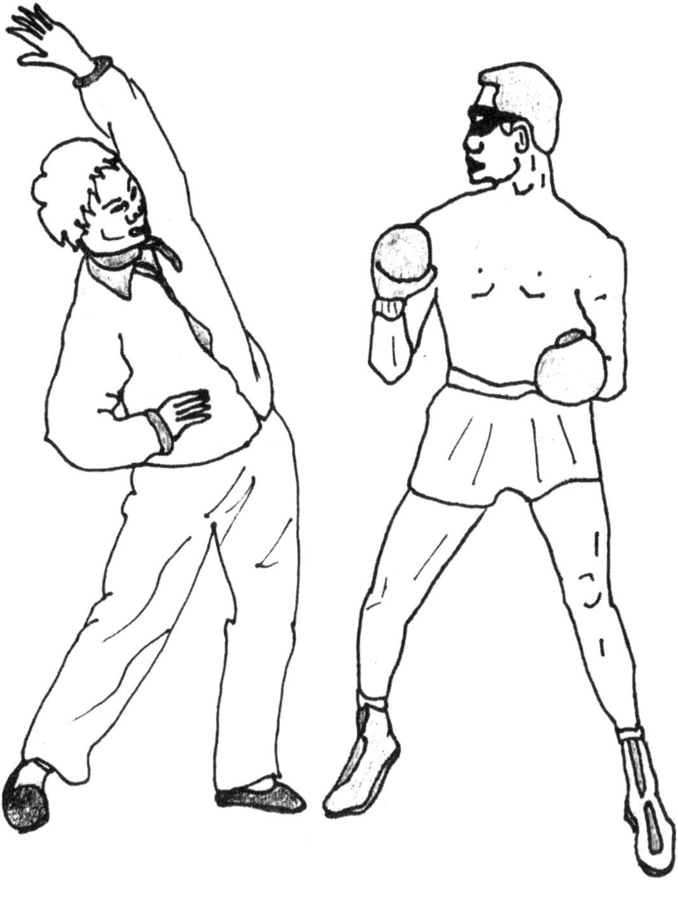

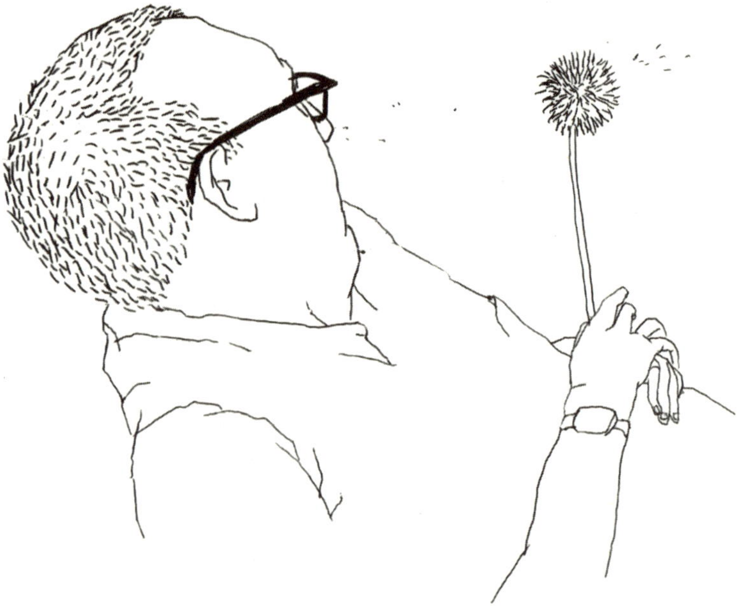

I

On her way to open the door, the woman glanced in the hallway mirror. She hated her face. It had two raised flesh-coloured moles and her nose was fat and her eye-lids puckered into rolls, as if sadness had collected there.

"I'm here about the room. I called earlier."

"Yes, come in."

The young woman took a step into the hallway.

"I'll show you round." They walked into the living room which had huge windows on both end walls. The light that morning shone bright and the flat was filled with warmth and sunshine. They climbed the stairs slowly to the upper level which had the bedrooms and bathroom and a small terrace on the back.

"This is the room for rent."

"Wow. It's huge."

"Yes."

FACE

by Hannah Griffiths

The young woman stepped into the bare room and walked around. She touched the mantlepiece and looked out of the back window which opened onto a corridor of back-gardens, like a long french avenue.

"And what about you?" She turned to the woman. "Do you work from home?"

The woman dipped her head and leant on the door jamb.

"Yes. I'm a graphic designer. My office is in my bedroom. There isn't much overspill."

"Right."

"Can I get you some tea?"

The young woman glanced out the window then looked back.

"No, it's fine. I should be going."

She moved as if to go.

As they reached the hallway the woman asked.

"So you like it?"

The young woman looked back along the hallway to the kitchen.

"I do. I do," she faced the woman and gave a tight smile. "I'll give you a ring later. I'm going to check out some other places."

"Ok."

She knew the young woman would never ring. Nobody had ever rung back even though the flat was in a desired location and was clean and freshly fitted out, a home to be proud of. That night the woman sat on the edge of her bed with her hands over her face and cried.

II

A couple of weeks later while checking the classifieds in the *Evening News* to make sure her advert for the room was still there, she noticed a small bold-boxed advert which read:

Unhappy with the way you look? We can help you out. Cosmetic surgery at competitive prices.

There was a phone number. She rang it and made enquiries. It would cost just £1000 for them to remove the moles, drain the eyelids and reduce the width of her nose. She had some space on a credit card which could pay for it. She made an appointment for the next week and that night found herself making a special meal, roasted meat with vegetables in careful sauces, a treat.

III

The 'clinic' was above a karaoke bar in Soho, on a stairway which had arrows pointing to 'Models' on the floors above. A wiry, dark-haired man, perhaps Eastern European, ushered her into the narrow waiting room, the kind of place mini-cab drivers might sit and wait for fares. He took the cash from her and led her into another room in which there was a dentist's chair. He put on a blue hospital robe and got out a box of hypodermic needles.

"I will inject you here and here." He drew some spots with a marker pen. "You won't feel anything but you might want to close your eyes. Some people no like seeing the knife, you know?" He raised his eyebrows and laughed a bit. The woman nodded slowly and shut her eyes and waited for the pin-pricks. He dabbed and injected and soon her face was fading away. The radio was caught at the edge of a station which played Classic hits—Rose Royce and Fleetwood Mac. The woman concentrated on the lyrics and the next hour and a half passed in silent agony as the man pushed and prodded at her face. She heard about impossible love and wishing for miracles and one song about a man who refused to take a woman back because she'd cheated on him with her best friend.

A cab brought her home and she hurried into her flat. In the hallway mirror, the mummified image stared back at her. The bandages stopped just at the white of her eyes so her tears were absorbed before they fell. She needed a drink but she had no straws and couldn't face going to the shop right now.

The experience had been horrific. The man hadn't even washed his hands. The place was so fly-by-night that there would be no recourse to a complaints board. It hadn't felt right what he did. What if the knife was dirty or he had breathed bad odour into a gap in her skin which would grow the germs. Why had she taken such a risk? Bandaged and bruised, she worried that she must have picked up infections. Did her misfortune—the room she could never rent, her loneliness, her lack of social group—hang so much on her misshapen face?

The woman lay down on the chaise-lounge and stared at the ceiling. Her face felt stiff and strange and not her own. She had been told to keep the bandages for two weeks and not be tempted to peek as any exposure to the air might cause a problem with the wounds. For once she was relieved that she had no friends or a lover so she could pass the weeks of shame alone.

IV

By the morning of the fourteenth day, the woman was in a bad state. Her dreams were filled with images of pus-ridden sores. In one of these nightmares, she had peeled off the bandages to find the man had cut off her entire face leaving only a mouth, gasping for air. Unable to face going outside since the operation, the woman was reduced to constructing meals from the dusty tins at the back of her cupboard—peaches and tinned vegetables. She drank water through the case of a ball-point pen, putting her finger over the hole. She didn't answer the phone which rang constantly with people wanting to see the room. And now the moment had come where she would see her botched up face and have to get treatment for infections and complications.

She took a bowl of water and cotton wool to her bedroom and sat at her dressing table. She undid the safety pin and let out a little yelp as she started unwrapping. She felt the temperature change on her face as the bandage thinned out. Then, the last layer of bandage fell away.

The woman stared at her reflection for a few seconds then laughed, the skin round her mouth stiff and out of practice. It was immediately clear that, indeed, the surgeon was a con-artist. But his con was to take the money and then push the patients numbed face about and prod and dig with cold objects. He had made no incisions. Her face was exactly the same. She put her hands on it to check and it was all there, all hers. She stood up and held her face and danced around the room. Realising she was starving, she grabbed her bag and keys and dashed out to her favourite sushi bar where she ordered miso soup and California rolls and asked for extra ginger.

V

"Hi there. Clare?"

"Yes, about the room?"

"Great. Come in."

"Sorry it had to be so early. I have to start work at nine. God," she stops and looks down the hallway to the kitchen. "What a great flat. And I love this road."

The woman takes Clare into the sitting room which is still in darkness. She pulls the rope which opens the curtains and the light bursts like a major chord.

"I'm getting such a good feeling here," said Clare.

The woman touches Clare's upper arm. "Let me show you your room. You'll love your room."

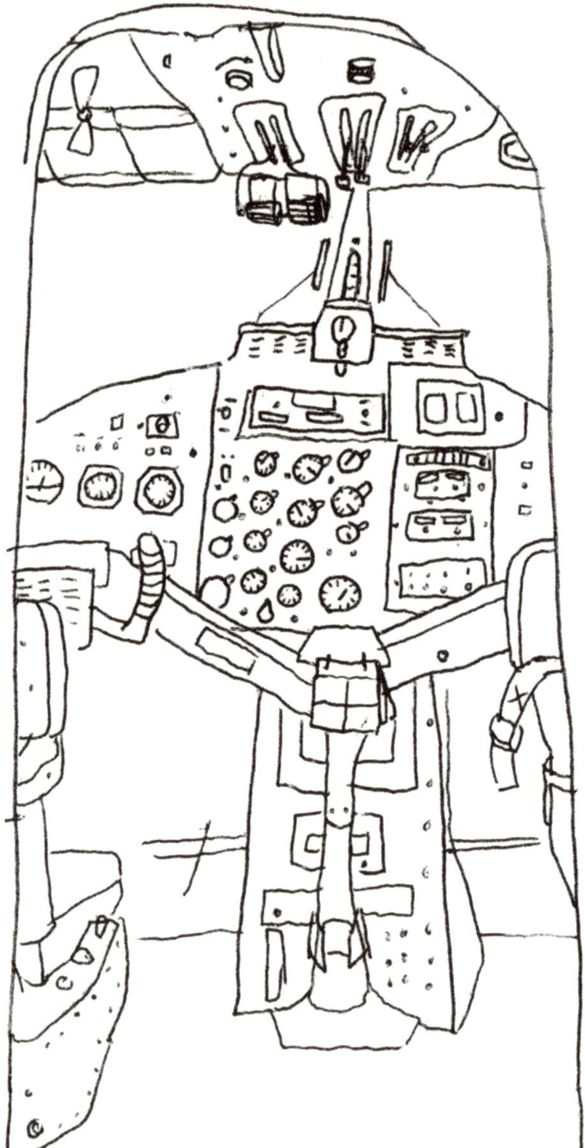

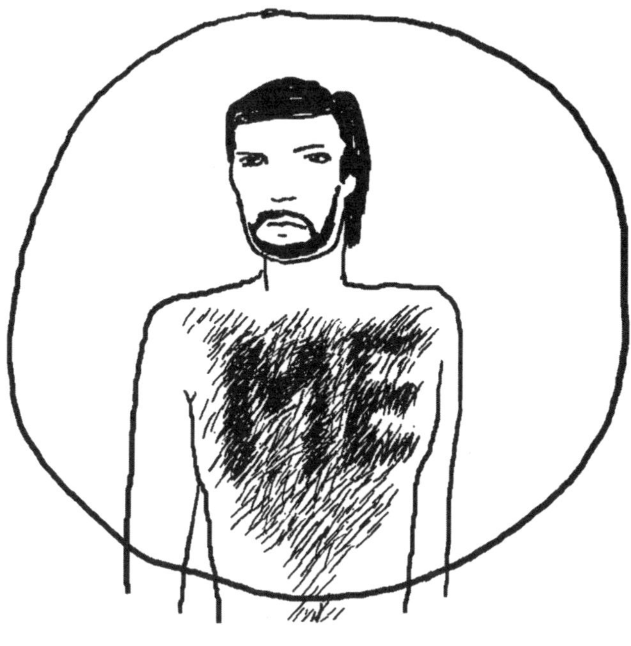
ME

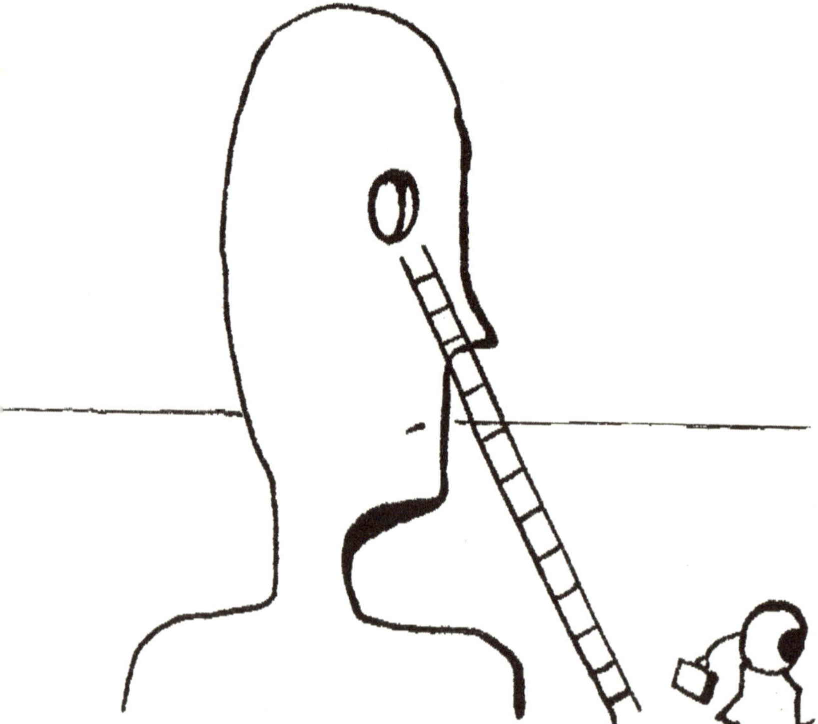

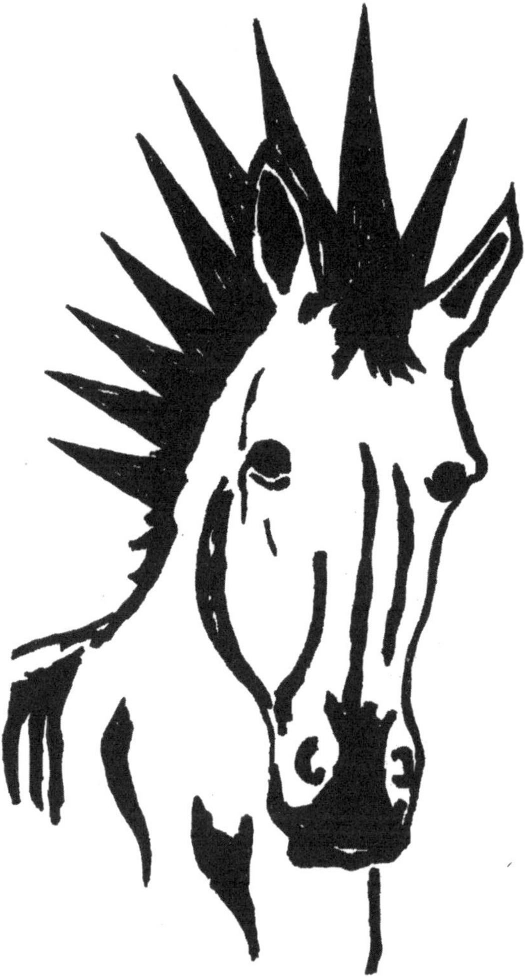

1977

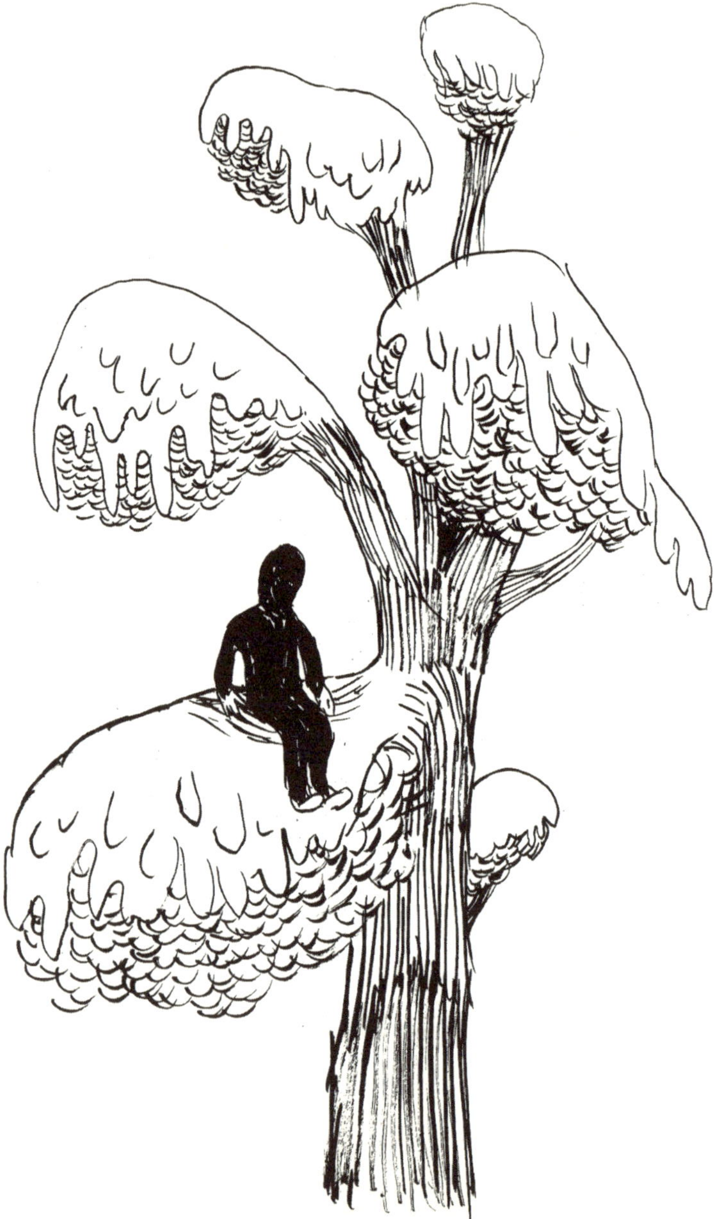

THE RADLOFF APPENDICES

by Jeff Johnson

The Decoy Wallet

I often leave a decoy wallet 15 inches inside of my cubicle. Like it's almost going somewhere on its own. I do that two weeks into any new job. Just sitting there on the carpet. There's nothing in it, except a business card I got from an ex-worm who sold gum-removing chemicals to amusement parks, and also maybe a one-dollar bill or two. Inside the dollar bill, usually, is a Post-It that says, "Don't spend it all in one place, Fuckstick." It's written in a greased navy ballpoint, pressed hard and scrawled in a shaky script that practically begs a crook to seal the deal and pocket it. Convinces them I deserve whatever's coming.

It's my S.O.B. test. It draws out any bastards in the midst. And are there *bastards*? Did Andy Capp like to get shithouse drunk? When the wallet's gone and someone starts giving me stinky looks—like *I'm* the asshole—then I know who the culprit is. Who I can't trust.

I'm always temping. Putting down stakes in some felt and steel sandstone-colored cubicle. Pressing palms.

Hitching my belt. Finding out where the toner's kept and who's getting sick of telling people about it. Getting inconvenienced by staff birthdays. Catching an earful of spittle while a guy prattles on about what Dave, or Ned or the Dinger did at with the tongs at the last company picnic. Or how he can't get a raise. I don't even bother saying wait a second, I'm just here to temp, friend. I just soak it all up.

<u>Further Clarification</u>
Why do I temp? Because I'm not a leader, according to today's standards and practices. The visions I have aren't anywhere *near* entrepreneurial in nature. They're more about the freshest new approaches in licking wounds. Retreating. Waiting to get dealt a losing hand.

What am I? More sponge than conduit. I'm often the last to know, and everything ends with me. *Anything*. Curls up around my feet and dies. I'm where people (see the Dinger, above) unload their problems after they've bored everyone else with them and are on their last-legs, withering, running out of steam. After the main anxiety of a situation has been squeezed, popped and spattered, I'm there for the sweeping up. For the bromide. I'm around to say, "The bright side is there wasn't any gasoline around. Coulda been much worse."
Example:
Jim, know what the doc said to me? [something about how

you gave up deodorant following your first blow job?] *He said its movie soda, plain and simple. See, Vicki, know how she loves to visit the theater? I've told you that before, I think. Yeah, and what I like about the movies is, I like snacks. Who doesn't? Right, Jimmy? Well, the movies means movie-sized beverages. Like 44 ounces or more. Right? Wouldn't be a decent value otherwise. Like a not-substantial soda at three—well, you get it. You're bright. Anyway, so, I sit down with a large waxy tumbler least three nights a week. Unless the movies are shit, which all of 'em are. But the drinks are all sugary, like Mountain Dew or something. Right? That shit tastes good though. F.U. to aspartame. That's what I say. And, now I've paid ten dollars for this theatrical experience, I ain't inclined to get up and take a piss and miss the visuals even thoughs I've consumed many, many ounces of soda. So, here I fiddle-fuck am, with a bladder full of whiz and half a soda left. And, just a sec-Jim,* [to interrupting coworker] *I am in the middle of a story? Hello?—Sorry, Jim—And pretty soon—this is what the doc says—one a my kidneys looks at the other kidney and the one kidney sorta half shrugs and says, Fuck this shit! And the other kidney looks at the first kidney and looks at itself and says, Well I don't wanna work, neither. And that's where all my problems start.*

<u>The Pond</u>

When Linda left, I started going to the pond on a more regular basis. Not that I care to fish, or am distracting myself with any koans of solitude or tranquility, but it was something I'd been missing. Guys piss and wail about being lonesome. The toughest guy you meet, you sit with an ear to him long enough and he's going to cry like a bitch. Unwrap all of his problems like a big hamburger, parting the bun from the meat, asking you to look underneath and maybe help flick off some excess cubed and/or diced onions. Where can you wipe your hand after that?

My least fav? Union guys. They're always seven or eight of them standing over a guy working a shovel telling him how he shoulda dug it. And you know they're also whining about what someone did to their tools, or the algebra of time-and-a-half, or the eyes their wife made at their brother on St. Paddy's Day. Holidays. People can't enjoy a holiday without melting down.

What I do up at the pond for the most part is my own business. I might just bring a pole and some cassettes up there and listen. I might not. It's not a formula. It's not zen. I've already repeated myself. There's not much more to say about this. Other than this: It used to be a party spot once.

Oh, and by the way, Linda and I were married in the era of gauze-lensed photography. When the word *promise* was adequate foreplay and lemon was acceptable as the *kicker* ingredient in a dessert. When cakes resembled tires. And your whims were allowed to swim freely inside of your body, without it meaning too much to anyone outside of you.

...And The Inverse of the Present?

Given enough time, there isn't anything I won't find inexcusable.

Dillard Square

My complex in Dillard Square consists of 18 one-bedroom pads in three stacks of six; situated on a buckled service road, adjacent to a more assertive, stop-lighted service road, in between the dying mall and the dead mall. Pigment-stripped toys in the parking lot. Chuckholes. Landlord in absentia. Rusted grills, keeled and forgotten. Walked away slowly from, backwards, while they were still smoking.

We got a lot of gourmets here, you know. Lots of guys who're gonna drink a few beers and grill up a hunk of salmon they embezzled from where ever offers a dining experience or embezzled groceries nearby. Then maybe they just work on the beers. Forget about the fish. Or torch it. Next thing they're maybe strangling each other. Or beating their starving kid with an old rotary telephone. A fallen branch. I stay out of it for the most part.

Am I pro-child abuse? Well, I don't keep score. I like to watch, I suppose. Till the faces pucker. Till they turn purple. Till it gets grossly unfair. Then what I do is call the cops. Turn on my scanner and get under the covers.

Shiver.

One Afternoon

One afternoon, I get a pounding on my door. The landlord's laminated paperwork insists that all barriers onsite remain wafer-thin. Just in case. I think the government gives him kickbacks on that, 'cause they need easy access to people in this income bracket. You never know when you'll have to swoop in on them, see what they're hoarding. Run some videotape of it. So I got a deadbolt and a little promise chain. I undo 'em. A guy from the building, not sure if I'll call him a neighbor or not says, "I got a free cot downstairs."

"I don't want it," I reach for the chain.

"Ain't for the taking," he snaps. "It's mine fair and square. I'm installing it for family visitor, er, visitors."

"Installing it, huh? Best of luck," I start to shut the door and he asks can I be of service and help him haul it up to 331. I ask myself if he is a fucking Ethiopian with pencil-thin arms. Because what's a cot? Eleven pounds?

He's onto to this discernable pause. He shatters it. "It's folded all fucked up!"

And then I understand he is in dire need of a break. I knew it from the first knock, I suppose, I knew it from the day they cut the tape and asked people to move in, but I let myself *understand* it now. That if there were a map of breaks, guy's been reading it upside down. That he's consistently navigated his head into a brick wall ever since the doctor slapped his behind and summoned him *next* in a long ancestry of dipshits.

I velcro my shoes and walk down. Our staircases are outdoors. The stairwells are Astroturfed traps. A plastic sign batters in the wind. You can see it from the highway. IF YOU LIVED HERE, YOU'D BE HOME BY NOW. If you lived here, your concept of home would need some massaging.

I realize I don't have my glasses. Doesn't matter in the end. He undoes some twine—with the same knife, I assume, that he uses to dissect his wobbly, thumbed grams of hashish or to cut free a fat trout with a hook jabbing out of its cheek—that runs through a broken lock-hole in his trunk. I grab an end of the thing and the guy grabs an end and we walk up the three flights of stairs.

"What'd ya knock on *my* door for?" I ask.

"I always see you peeking out your blinds in the daytime," he says. He's bent over breathing. "Thanks, bro."

About an hour later my door starts jiggling in its frame again. It's him. Brian. His impression: We're best friends now. Once a day gets the Good Sam routine from me. Twice a day and he's a fucking nozzle-nosed creep. This is the sour part of me that eventually became the whole of me. Eventually forced Linda to say, "You're not even you anymore."

I laugh about that because her next sentence was, "Do you even know that about yourself?" She said it clipped. Hastily. Like I had one hand on my nose and was about to sink deep into a lake.

"Which *you* do you mean?" I asked. Those were the days I liked sleeping on the couch. It was kind of like a night off, if you know what I mean. Do you?

So Brian. Okay.

"You're taking my nap away," I yell in the general direction of the outside wall. The fucker had my nap in a half-nelson and he was walking it around. Showing it off. Saying unpleasant things about its mother. I'm on the sofa, please. I'm putting away a little yogurt and reading the classifieds, with my eyes shut, please. Dreaming of a thicker door. I rustle the papers and tromp to the saxophone reed that is my door.

"Thought maybe I'd wet your whistle," he yells through the door.

I'm afraid to find out what that entails. "Meaning what?" Is any lube involved? Is it something that might be broadcast on the internet.

"Up for a cold beverage?" he asks. That changed the tenor of the situation by a hair.

"Let's say *drink*," I reach for my windbreaker. "Beverage has too many syllables."

We drive to the Stuckey's. Known primarily for it's coffee and poor lighting, the Stuckey's where we live serves alcohol. Loopholes. Our county fiddles good and long on loopholes, adds a tax, and then we dive straight into them. Stuckey's has three U-shaped bars and a genderless smart ass doling out libations inside each station. Well, not a smart ass. Just someone who wants to get your goat. Someone who thinks maybe that for a dollar fifty and your goat, you should get a beer and a headache, no backs.

Brian gets me a beer and I already know where this is going. Favor number two is forever.

"Georgette has some of my possessions," Brian says by way of nothing. I admire that he doesn't struggle this into our chat. He drops it like I'm on first names with his kin.

"But *not* the cot." I gulp my beer and point the neck of it at him as an exclamation point.

"Yes, but she does have something I need back."

"Your heart?" I groan. "Listen, I had the pleasure once of working the returns desk at the mall after Christmas," I say.

"Meaning what?"

"Meaning my attention span for sob stories is short—"

"I'm only wondering—"

"Let me finish," I say. I see the panic in his face. "I'll listen as long as I can. Then I might punch you."

"I just want to see my kid."

"This is some drink, Brian."

The Sleepy Nun

We got a twelve pack for the road and forty minutes later we were on the most depressing stretch of Cty HH, past the Menard's. Past the Ringing Siren Bar & Grille, and up into the Sleepy Nun efficiencies. I wanted to see when things would get better. I could always wait it out on the sofa. I figured maybe the sofa was waiting it out on me—keeping me, with the help of *White Shadow* reruns—from achieving much more than tattling on the drunk neighbors, or looking at a photograph of Linda that a hunk of yellowing Scotch tape was holding hostage inside of the medicine cabinet.

"Inside unit 8 is my ex-wife, my child and a lottery ticket that is a certified winner," Brian snuckled. The road ale dripped from his mustache. His face was lit green from the dashboard. His calloused mitt was on the shifter.

"I don't do kidnappings, Brian. Do I look like a fucking kidnapper?"

"Relax. I'm not the kind of guy, if you couldn't tell, who wants the kid back." The car idled on the gravel. Twenty yards away a little yellow light glowed inside of an efficiency.

"Good."

"At least not permanently."

"See? Slow down. Slow down. Jesus."

"Wha' who do you think the cot was for, man?"

"Let's just focus on the window-peeping and maybe that lotto ticket, Brian" I said. "How do you know she hasn't cashed it?" I asked.

"I don't."

"How does anyone like you ever win?"

"Just shut up," Brian said. "Just have a look for the kid, and if they're asleep, I wanna take a look at him. That's all."

The Sleepy Nun was an old whitewashed wooden motel that had been built when the town was supposedly unspooling and expanding this-a-way. Later, a vote was held and a man in a wool tuxedo stood at a platform with a halo of dying oak leaves falling around his head and announced that growth had halted. The crowd harrumphed.

There was a chapel (caved in) and these clapboard huts were used to discreetly house delinquent nuns in the 1960s. The ones who opposed the Vietnam invitational. The ones who might not wear undies under all the cloth. The ones who let you know what stank and where you could put it. After a stretch, the nuns either escaped or got pregnant and the rest of the rooms were parceled out to tenants who figured that maybe the bill collectors would never find them there. Of course they were wrong, and subsequently a steady stream of them were beating a retreat to the next batch of dwellings to wait it out.

I got out of the car to have a look. I walked across the gravel. Tried to think of a theme song. Something to get me going. Keep me motivated. Keep me from feeling so guilty about looking in a lady's window. I half figured the whole deal was a set-up to konk me on the head, but I didn't take that seriously, because what? I was better than Brian? I had a wallet full of hundreds? He *wasn't* that dumb. Neither one of us would be written about when we were dead.

Inside the screen door, I could hear a box fan wheezing in a pathetic attempt at cooling things off, or at least setting a metronome, a rhythm that would keep the hut from closing in on itself. Make it inhabitants believe it might be a heartbeat, that the house was saying, "We're all in this together."

I could see the ex-of-Brian, passed out, finally, not

from booze or intoxicants, but frustration probably, crosswise on top of the diapered child, pinning it gently to a square of Astroturf. Both were snoring loudly. A string-challenged ukulele lay near the bodies, surrendered. The toddler had a death grip on a hair brush. There had been, most likely, a bath and a subsequent struggle. Someone had been trying to get someone else pretty for something. The place reeked of baby aspirin and boiled noodles.

Long story short, I left Brian and the car running out on the gravel. I took my time and eventually the rumble of the engine retracted and disappeared down the highway. Coward. I went in and examined the ticket. It was nothing, really. I shook some shoulders awake, made some introductions and insinuated my hands into a can of Folgers. Did some explaining. I dropped everything (okay, there wasn't much to drop) for as long as I could and loved this mother and child. We lived as a family. The kid was always sticky and candied himself to the living room floor. There was a map of stains the dog was snooting at—a strait of punches and puddings, cheesings, blackened yogurt gloppings—from the kitchen island to the television set. We were permanently late for a parade. My naps were again pummeled, hidden and quarantined away from me.

There are those first awkwardly energetic months when you steal a loved one away from someone else. When you feel like a fucking *tiger*, and you take a certain glee recanting and condescending to how it was all, sadly, deserved. And sure, Brian got very sore. Threw pans of hot water on us. Had our somewhat healthy Pomeranian put to sleep on Halloween. Threw acid at the Dillard Square security guard. Ended up making obscene and forward phone calls to his own attorney's wife. Did his time, came back with odd tribal tattoos, and intense, yet oddly ungracious apologies.

How the Wheels Came Off

I abandoned the temping life—my little hate-cloud of irresponsibility—and took on consistent work, once again, at the mall in an embarrassing role for any man: the Sweatpants Fairy. Being in love, it does amazing things to shame. To dignity. It sends it scurrying into caves. Under couches. I sat in a kiosk collecting used athletic wear for needy families who wanted to get into shape. Who had a 5k or a lay-up drill around the corner. We all pretended—to the point of appropriate costumery—that we were going on high alert against the crippling obesity epidemic, when in fact booths within a belly-length from us were still offering More Toppin' Than Pretzel boats. Vats of melted *anything*. We had a splendid life together for a moment. The kid, too.

In time, though, the kid got to the age where it sucked maybe to have dear old dad rounding up fatigued gym shorts. To hear maybe, from a friend that your new apparel was most likely once their second cousin's who gave up wrestling to learn guitar. Somewhere around that time, the wife caught on, too. Or I caught on to her, rather. Or maybe I caught onto myself. But I wouldn't admit it and I'm not really owning up to it now. We quietly decided on separate everything.

<u>Final Thoughts</u>

The number of suicides in my county, in my polyp of a community, has never been unusually high. Maybe twice a year, a guy in financial hot water might run a garden hose from his exhaust pipe into the back window of his sedan, after putting his church clothes on and penning a farewell note on his wife's lilac stationery. A teenager might hang himself on the party hill after getting poor marks. You might think, after hearing these joyous tales, that I would give offing myself some serious thought. And I do give it serious thought. As in, how in the fuck could they do *that* to themselves? That's precisely when I turn the obit page to the brain-screech of the letters section in an effort to catalog who feels wronged and how they verbalize it, or I palm blindly underneath the newspaper for the remote, just to further identify what else has been screwed up. And how much louder I can suck my teeth in an empty room.

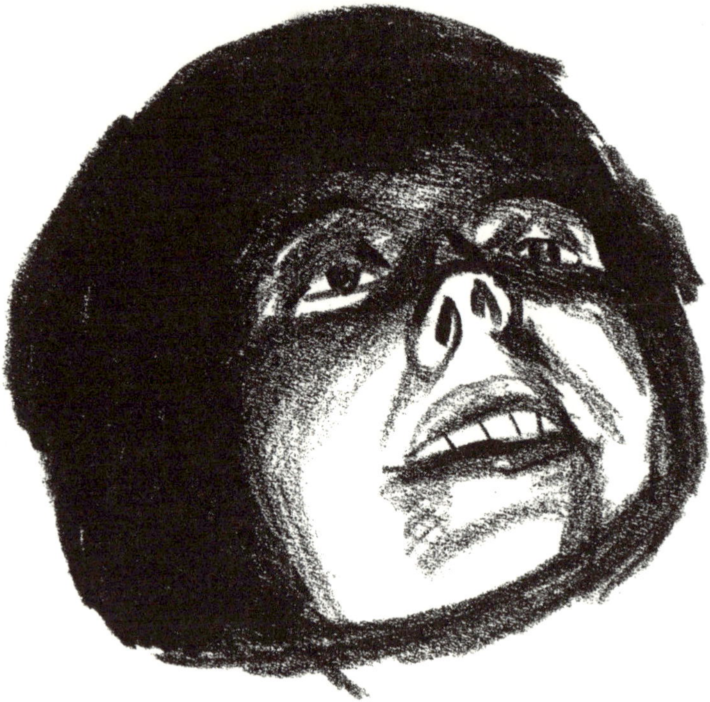

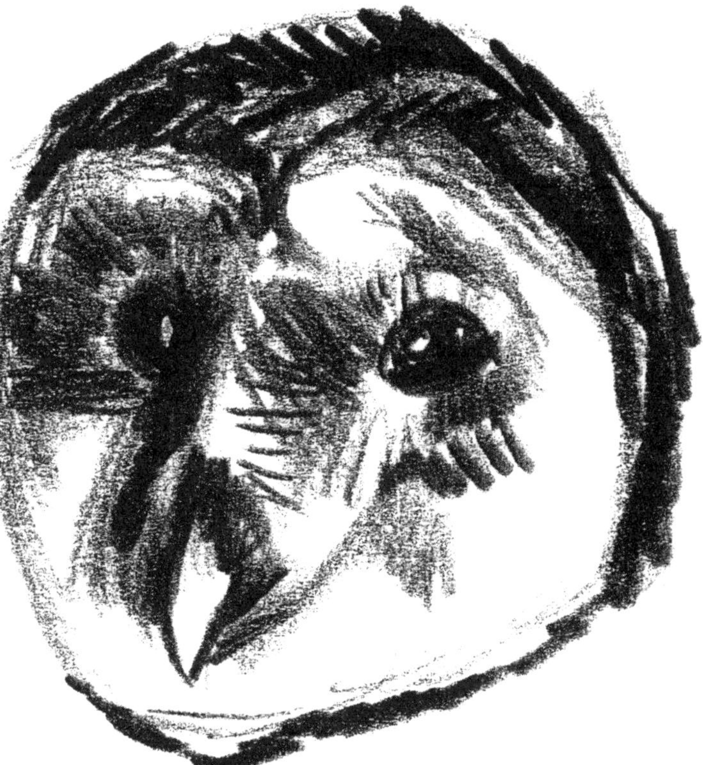

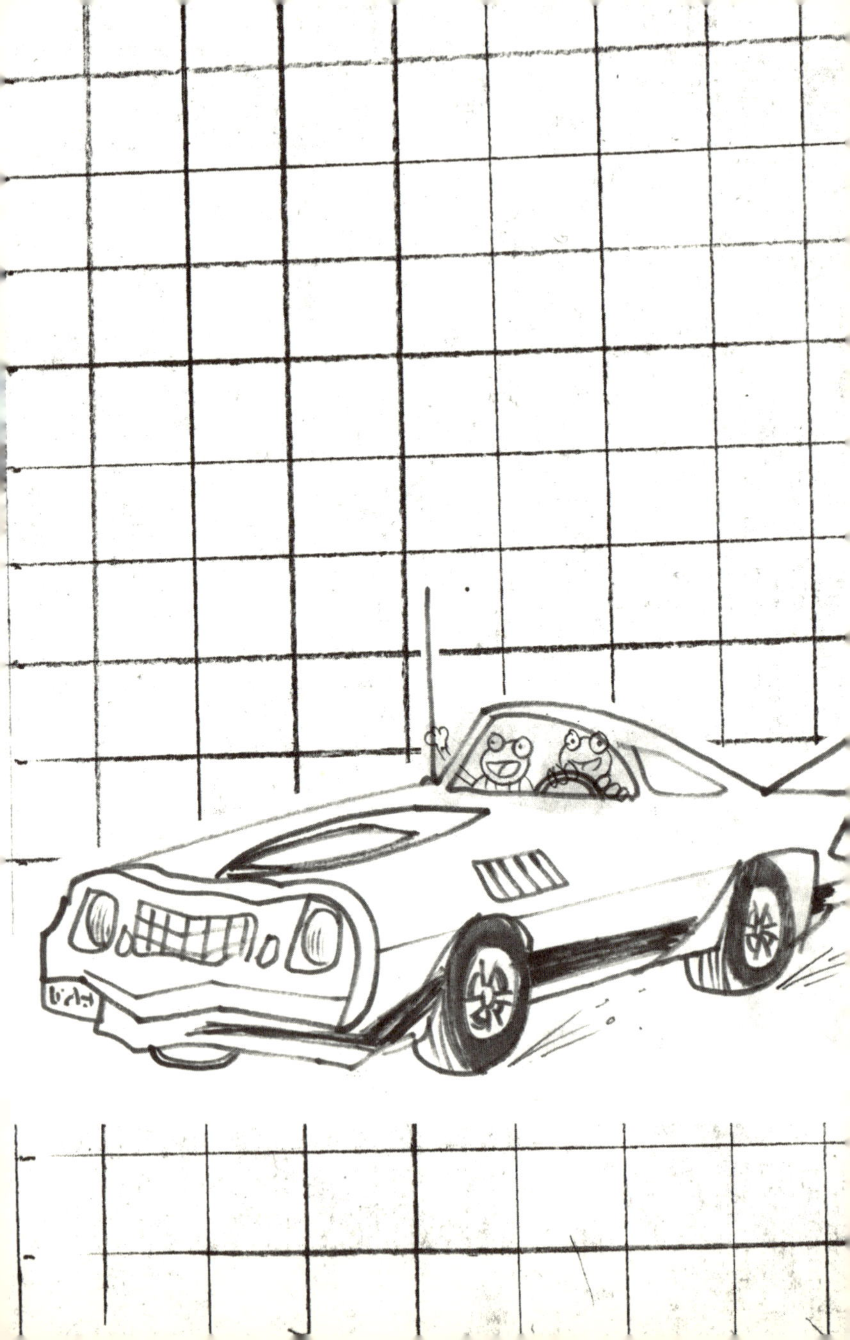

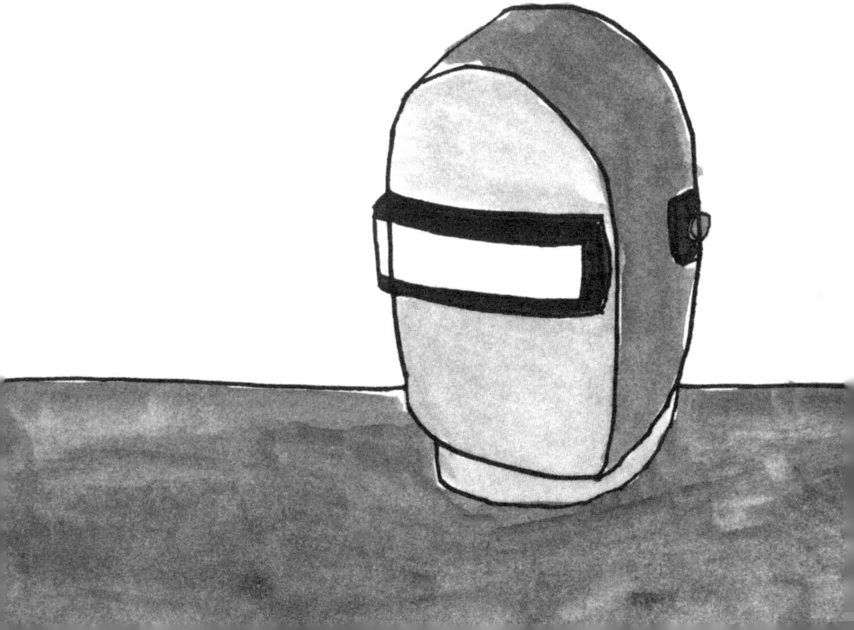

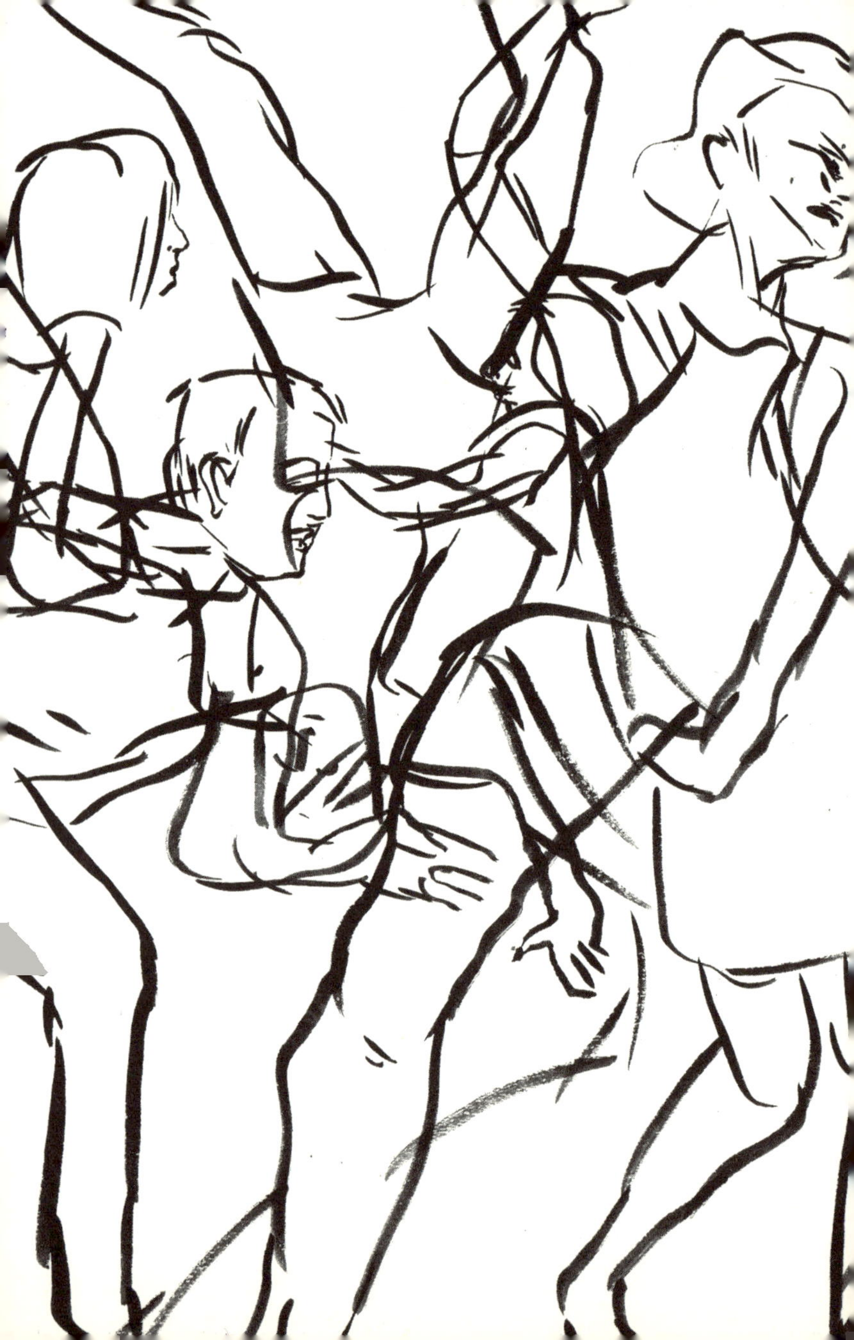

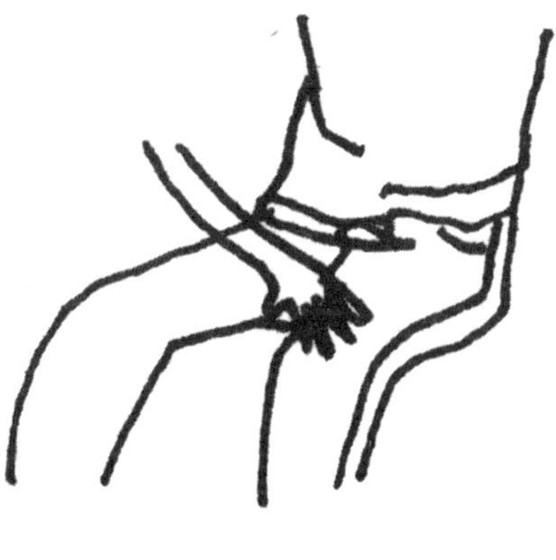

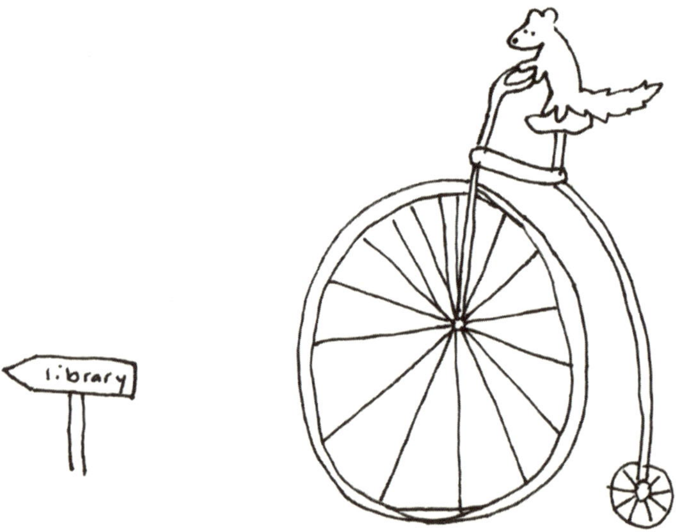
library

This Cloudless Weight is a masterwork of aching beauty and sore truth. With deer-like gentleness and bovine patience, this is a book that compiles the histories that twist and jerk us. Set amid various wars, though mostly World Wars I through II, *This Cloudless Weight* tells of the carrot-haired, apple-cheeked, banana-legged, mango-footed farmboys churned into the fields of France. And of the cunning, rutting hogs bred especially to sniff them out. And of the time-worn, teetering omas that lay them end to end. And of the daredevil cyclists leaping rows of the fallen, tears filling their brightly starred helmets. (In addition to those characters, the book is lousy with carvers and tailors and gardeners and photographers and nurses and nuns and smithies and sappers and forensic something-or-others.)

NEW FALL LIST

by Nathan Whitlock

This Cloudless Weight is a powerful evocation of the tempestuousness of place and the unctuousness of destiny. With words muscular and tender that speak of memory as if of a bubbling rash hidden by sleeves and cream, *This Cloudless Weight* transports us through dangerous waterways, calming us with hard-won humour, but failing to warn us of the animatronic sharks. It tattoos self-spun fictions onto our backs. It is a tale of rapid visions, of fragmentary violence, as if told by a stuttering auctioneer. It lobs ideas at our minds and demands that we think fast.

This Cloudless Weight hemorrhages beautiful prose, written with a painterly eye, a carpenterly jaw, a salesmanly wrist. Readers lose themselves in the text like children in a ball room. Time and time again, the book's lush imagery and poetic stylings evoke the intricate designs and enveloping comfort of patterned wallpaper—each word placed with the care of a jeweller, each sentence like the strum of a stolen guitar, each paragraph beautiful from ten steps back. Like the slow maturation of our musical tastes, *This Cloudless Weight* dispenses with the stony and brittle emotions of youth and becomes all jazz, jazz, jazz. It is the hot madness of a poetry slam and the cool calm of cottage water. Within such a human theatre as this, you can hear the gentle actors backstage, warming up, doing scales, adjusting moustaches.

This Cloudless Weight provides us with the grace of private passage, with legroom and extra seats for our delicate, blind pets, too old for storage. Longing and loss are given equal time, and the sorts of desires that infect us are well-represented, too. This is a book that sews together the horizon's clouds and wipes fingerprints off the moon. It holds a beating, burping human heart to the light. It contains many shocks of recognition and furtive spurts of truth, as when we first found those magazines in the woods.

This Cloudless Weight investigates troubling occurrences—with its questions and shadowy deductions, the book interrogates us in a cold, bare room, probing for gaps and inconsistencies, forcing a confession, bringing us coffee in a cup. It is sheer malevolence. It is hard nails and soft rain. Readers will read *This Cloudless Weight* and be changed from the readers they were to the readers they are.

Hand-stitched vellum manuscript available.

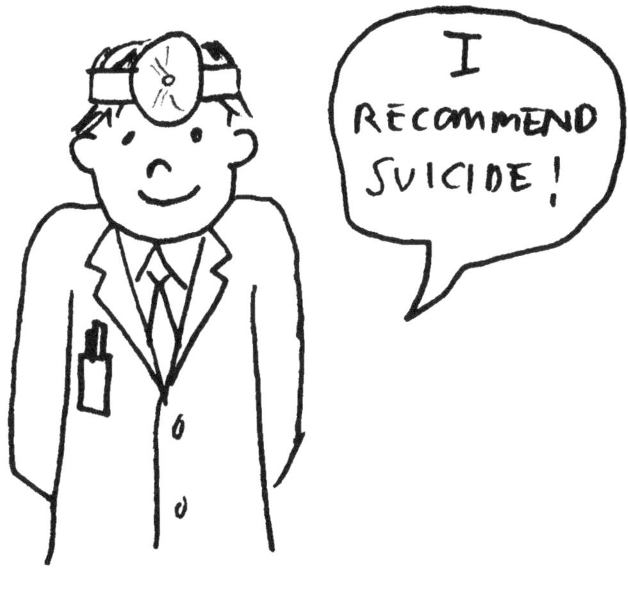
I RECOMMEND SUICIDE!

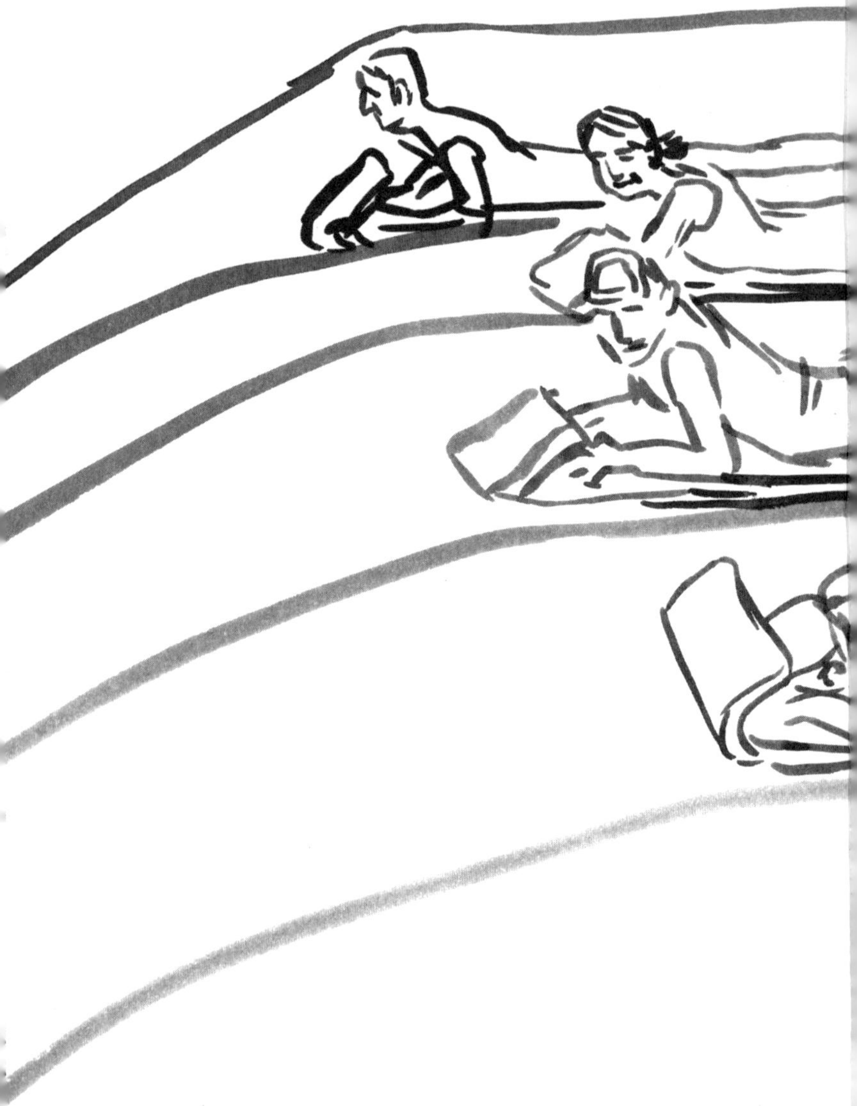